NEW PENGUIN SHAKESPEARE
GENERAL EDITOR: T. J. B. SPENCER
ASSOCIATE EDITOR: STANLEY WELLS

WILLIAM SHAKESPEARE

*

TWELFTH NIGHT

EDITED BY
M. M. MAHOOD

PENGUIN BOOKS

Penguin Books Ltd, Harmondsworth, Middlesex, England
Penguin Books, 625 Madison Avenue, New York, New York 10022, U.S.A.
Penguin Books Australia Ltd, Ringwood, Victoria, Australia
Penguin Books Canada Ltd, 2801 John Street, Markham, Ontario, Canada L3R 1B4
Penguin Books (N.Z.) Ltd, 182–190 Wairau Road, Auckland 10, New Zealand

—

This edition first published in Penguin Books 1968
Reprinted 1971, 1972, 1973, 1974,
1976, 1977, 1978, 1979, 1980, 1981

—

—

Made and printed in Great Britain
by Richard Clay (The Chaucer Press) Ltd,
Bungay, Suffolk
Set in Monotype Ehrhardt

CONTENTS

INTRODUCTION

AMONG the high-rise buildings and packed car parks of present-day London there are a very few places where it is possible to stand, look round, and say 'This is what Shakespeare saw.' The hall of the Middle Temple is one such place. True, much of the decoration of its beautiful interior is only a replica of what was destroyed in the Second World War. Yet a sense of the past is very strong here. The reason is perhaps that for four centuries Middle Temple Hall has continued to be put to the use for which it was built. Benchers and law-students still eat their dinners under its hammerbeam roof, as they did in Elizabethan days, when the Inns of Court were the country's third university, attended by hundreds of young men who had come to London to learn as much of the law as was required for the administration of the Queen's affairs and of their own estates.

On 2 February 1951, the restoration of Middle Temple Hall was celebrated by a performance of *Twelfth Night*. The date chosen was an anniversary. All but three and a half centuries earlier, on 2 February 1602 - Candlemas Day - Shakespeare's company, and presumably Shakespeare among them, had acted *Twelfth Night* in the same hall. Regrettably, we know nothing of the way the play was staged on that occasion. The actors may have taken advantage of the magnificent screen, already darkening after thirty years of use, which stood across the entrance to the hall and which would have afforded them a setting very similar to the back wall of the Elizabethan public playhouse. A platform stage could have been built to the height of the base of the screen's pilasters, leaving ample room for entrance through the two lofty arched doorways. These were presumably curtained – the present doors date from the Restoration – and may have served not only for entrances and exits but also for the box-tree (with three heads bobbing up above the curtain rail) in Act II, scene 5, and for the dark house, with Malvolio's hand groping pathetically through the opening, in Act IV, scene 2 – unless, that is, the company brought a box-tree and a solid property 'dark house' with them. We have no way of knowing; but we do know how the play was received on that night in 1602 by one member of the audience, a barrister called John Manningham:

> *At our feast* (Manningham noted in his diary), *we had a play called* Twelfth Night *or* What You Will*; much like the* Comedy of Errors, *or* Menaechmi *in Plautus, but most like and near to that in Italian called* Inganni. *A good practice in it to make the steward believe his lady widow was in love with him, by counterfeiting a letter as from his lady in general terms, telling him what she liked best in him, and prescribing his gesture in smiling, his apparel, etc. And then when he came to practise, making him believe they took him to be mad.*

No spectator can relish the effect of a comedy in isolation from the rest of the audience round him, and Manningham's enjoyment must have been widely shared. The players had brought to the feast a thoroughly festive play. *Twelfth Night* was conceived for a time of pleasure: this is the clue to the play's special mood and flavour which set it apart from – many would say above – Shakespeare's other comedies.

Masques and revels, such as the plays Sir Andrew

delights in 'altogether', were a feature of life at Court, the Inns of Court, and the Universities for some three months of the year. This tradition of winter feasting was older than Christianity, but by Shakespeare's time it had become associated with a number of Church festivals extending from St Andrew's Day, or even from Hallowe'en a month earlier, through the twelve days of Christmas to Candlemas and so on to Shrovetide, just before Lent. Special private performances of plays were often a part of these festivities. Between Christmas Day 1597 and Candlemas 1598, for example, the students of the Middle Temple enjoyed two comedies – one of them followed by dancing – three masques, and a number of other entertainments of a make-believe kind. Sometimes the make-believe embraced the whole feast: a Lord of Misrule, attended by a fool or jester, could usurp all normal authority in the social group – as he did at St John's College, Oxford, in the winter of 1607 to 1608. So at the Middle Temple in 1602 feast and farce must have blended together in the 'civil misrule' of Sir Toby and his companions; the killjoy upstart Malvolio was placed at the mercy of Sir Toby much in the same way as crusty benchers had to submit, during the feasting, to the caprices of young law-students. Even the music with which the play opens could have been part of the after-dinner music provided by a consort, or small orchestra, in the gallery of the hall; and the song with which it ends is in the nature of a jig and could lead on to further music.

The music of *Twelfth Night* provides much more than the festive framework to the play. Two kinds of music are integral to the comedy itself. On the one hand, there are the straight love songs, 'O mistress mine' and 'Come away, death'; on the other, snatches of songs that satirize love or are sung in a way that burlesques sentiment: 'My lady is unkind, perdy'; 'Farewell, dear heart, since I must needs be gone'; and the ballad of Susanna and the Elders, which reflects the impropriety of Malvolio's passion for Olivia. This is a deliberate contrast, basic to the nature of a festive play. The union of romance and satire, of poetry and wit, in *Twelfth Night*, corresponds to a union found in festive rites wherever they are performed in the world: a union between the invocation of nature's plenty and the ritual abuse of powers that may work against her blessings. *Twelfth Night* is a festive play not just because it was written for a feast and has a high-spirited plot, but rather because it is in itself a kind of saturnalia to invoke the festive virtues and to exorcize the killjoy powers.

Chief among these festive virtues is the capacity to enjoy oneself. John Donne once told a Jacobean congregation that God loved a cheerful taker quite as much as He loved a cheerful giver. This would have struck Shakespeare's audience as sound doctrine; any spoilsport who, at a time when food was getting short, days cold, and work burdensome, refused the opportunities for plentiful food and drink, fires and entertainment, which were offered by the Church's calendar deserved, in their view, to be baited like Malvolio. At its simplest level, then, *Twelfth Night* defends people's right to cakes and ale. But it has a deeper concern with present mirth. When Olivia vows to season a brother's dead love with her tears for seven years – the very image suggests winter, since the Elizabethans had to make do with salted food until the spring pastures were ready – she is failing to understand that there is a time for everything: 'A time to weep, and a time to laugh; a time to mourn and a time to dance.' Human life, like nature's, has its due seasons (II.4. 38–9) –

For women are as roses whose fair flower,
Being once displayed, doth fall that very hour.

So too when Feste tries to rally Olivia out of her melancholy (I.5.46–7) with the words

As there is no true cuckold but calamity, so beauty's a flower,

he deftly hints at her folly in mourning when she should be marrying. And Orsino, for his part, also fails to seize the present time when he lies back on sweet beds of flowers and performs his wooing by proxy.

In contrast to such misusers of time, Viola and Sebastian grasp him by the forelock. We first hear of Sebastian in the story of how he survived shipwreck – 'Courage and hope both teaching him the practice' (I.2.13). Viola is just as tenacious of life. As soon as she reaches land she begins to make resourceful plans for her survival and safety. The whole-hearted zest with which she flings herself into the role of Orsino's page is just the frame of mind that masques and revels call for. And when Olivia becomes infatuated, Viola adjusts rapidly to the new situation, simply trusting that an opportunity will present itself (II.2.40) for setting matters to rights:

O time, thou must untangle this, not I!

This willingness to trust all to time has another aspect. It is not only a readiness to seize opportunities when they offer themselves, but it is also a readiness to bide the time when it is necessary to do so. In this connexion it is interesting to notice that both Viola's longsuffering and her image of Patience on a monument are foreshadowed in the Prologue to the Italian play of *Gl'Ingannati*, which we shall see was one of Shakespeare's sources for his plot: 'Two lessons above all you will take away with you: how great is the power of chance and good fortune in affairs of love; and how great too in them is the value of long-enduring patience accompanied by good counsel.' As Shakespeare dispensed with all the parents and mentors in his source, good counsel in the play comes only from Feste; but patience, and the readiness to take whatever opportunities time offers, are Viola's shining virtues. They are her brother's virtues too. Sebastian's sprint to the altar with Olivia is not, as is sometimes suggested, a crude device for making the broad plots of Shakespeare's sources 'respectable'; it shows rather that Sebastian recognizes 'the power of chance and good fortune in affairs of love', and is as ready as his sister to make the best of opportunity.

Twelfth Night extols the cheerful giver as well as the cheerful taker: generosity is celebrated alongside the festive virtue of a right opportunism. From antiquity onwards, present-giving has been an important part of most festivities, and a surprising number of presents, in the form of money and jewels, change hands during the play's action. In all these benefactions, Shakespeare maintains a distinction of which 'under-developed' societies are much more aware than are developed ones, between the gift that is a real love-token – like the Roman honey and gold – and the gift that is mere payment or bribe. There is no generosity, nothing indicative of the *generosus*, or man of breeding, about Sir Andrew's attempt to buy off his opponent with the gift of his horse, or about Malvolio's promise of reward if Feste will help him to pen, paper, and a candle. Feste is especially sensitive to the spirit in which gifts are bestowed. When the Duke Orsino, whose appetite for Feste's music is quickly surfeited, drops a coin into his hand with a cool 'There's for thy pains' (II.4.66), he gets from Feste, the artist to whom payment is at once a necessity and an unreality, the equally cool retort: 'No pains, sir. I take pleasure in singing, sir.'

In contrast to such ungenerous giving stands the generosity of Sebastian, Antonio, Viola, and ultimately of Olivia. Sebastian does not know how he can repay Antonio for his goodness; he dreads making him a 'bad recompense' or shuffling him off 'with such uncurrent pay' as mere thanks. For Sebastian is himself a warm-hearted enough person to see that Antonio's entrustment to him of all his money is the least part of his generosity. Antonio gives himself away with his gold, and in consequence Sebastian's apparent ingratitude wounds him deeply. But of course what has really happened is that Antonio has mistaken the disguised Viola for Sebastian; and she rebuffs his appeal with what seems to him the ultimate hypocrisy – a speech in condemnation of ingratitude. This speech is very much in character. First among Viola's unrehearsed words to Olivia (I.5.181) is a protest at Olivia's miserly hoarding of her natural gifts – 'what is yours to bestow is not yours to reserve'. Nor can Viola understand the temperament that (lines 231–2)

will lead these graces to the grave,
And leave the world no copy.

The warmth of her protestations on Orsino's behalf (lines 241–2) –

O, such love
Could be but recompensed!

awakens at last a warmth of feeling in Olivia and then of course the complications of comedy begin; but through them all Shakespeare keeps before us the two festive virtues of opportunism and generosity, as they are epitomized in Olivia's own words (III.1.153):

Love sought, is good; but given unsought, is better.

The play evokes the festive virtues without preaching them. Nor is there any Christmas Book bonhomie, any exhortation to be jolly and join in, about this play with a Christmas title. In trying to define the mood of *Twelfth Night* as a festive play we should not look forward, anachronistically, to the cosy merry-making of Dingley Dell, but rather backwards in time to the Feast of Fools and other medieval revels. For in these survived, almost to Shakespeare's own day, the second main aspect of ancient festivities: their 'ritual abuse of hostile spirits'. Once we have grasped the spell-like, incantatory nature of such abuse, we can perhaps begin to respond to the baiting of Malvolio as an Elizabethan audience may have responded. It is not to be thought of as heartless practical joking, but as a form of exorcism; and this response lends piquancy to the scenes in which Malvolio is actually treated as a man 'possessed'.

The device used against Olivia's steward is only one aspect of the play's satirical character. Everywhere in *Twelfth Night* we find the topsyturvy inversions typical of the Feast of Fools, when folly reigned in the seat of wisdom in order to show up the foolishness of those who counted themselves wise, and when the confusions of the masquerade brought home to all the truth that, in sober daily life, we know neither our own identities nor the identities of our neighbours. Folly, which walks the orb like the sun, permeates the language of the play: Sir Andrew, a bumpkin knight, recalls the good country saying that fools have wit enough to keep themselves dry; and every fool, according to Feste's song, knows how to make use of opportunity when it calls. Much of the play sustains Blake's belief that if the fool would persist in his folly he would become wise. Olivia runs mad for the love of 'Cesario', yet this alienation is really a discovery of her own repressed instincts. The behaviour of Feste and Sir Andrew, and finally of Olivia herself, seems sheer lunacy to Sebastian, but he decides to do as the rest in this mad place – and immediately finds happiness as Olivia's husband. Malvolio is led a long dance through midsummer madness to the sober, reproachful letter he writes, not as Count Malvolio, but as Olivia's faithful steward. Significantly, Feste has no part in Malvolio's gulling until the point at which he can begin to lead him back to normalcy.

Just as in *Much Ado About Nothing*, where the 'shallow fools' bring to light what wisdom could not discover, clarification is reached in *Twelfth Night* through massive delusions. This is very much in keeping with the spirit of Elizabethan Christmas revels, with their masquerades and carnival-like disguises. Shakespeare perhaps saw in such mummery a process at work similar to the illusions of the theatre which help us to discover the truth of what we are. Accordingly, *Twelfth Night* is a play composed of deceptions – *inganni*. Olivia and Orsino are self-deceivers: the one in her delusion that she can live like an imperial votaress, the other in thinking he really loves Olivia; in fact, the first time in the play he comes face to face with her he is so disconcerted that he immediately starts to quarrel with her. Malvolio thinks Olivia is in love with him, Sir Andrew thinks he can marry Olivia, Olivia thinks she can marry 'Cesario'. Antonio thinks Viola is Sebastian, Sir Andrew and Sir Toby think Sebastian is Viola, Malvolio thinks Feste is Sir Topas. Viola thinks Sir Andrew a redoubtable swordsman and he thinks the same of her. And yet through all these confusions clarification and self-knowledge are reached, just as a masquerade releases people from their everyday inhibitions and enables them to discover themselves.

Twelfth Night, or the Feast of the Epiphany, itself

symbolic of the readiness to bring gifts and to receive a great joy, was also the last feasting day of the Christmas season. At Oxford, in 1603, the Prologue to a 'Twelfth Night merriment' pleaded with his audience –

> *This is the night, night latest of the twelve;*
> *Now give us leave for to be blithe and frolic.*
> *Tomorrow we must fall to dig and delve . . .*

Shakespeare's *Twelfth Night* too is a holiday entertainment in which we are made aware of the proximity of the non-holiday world. This is the last of Shakespeare's happy comedies, and when he creates another Fool, it is to drive him out into the wind and the rain. In *King Lear*, the worst cruelty is found withindoors. In *Twelfth Night*, however, we are still secure in the festive hall, in what has been called an evergreen world in contrast to the self-renewing green world of a pastoral comedy such as *As You Like It*. Yet even here the leader of the revels, Feste, is threatened (I.5.105): 'your fooling grows old'. The fear of being turned away causes Malvolio's sneer (lines 71–2) – 'Infirmity, that decays the wise, doth ever make the better fool' – to rankle for a long time in Feste's thoughts. Nor does Feste's 'love of having', the workaday virtue of prudence, belong by right to the holiday world; but then patrons will not always be expansive and generous. And outside the holiday world, love is not always generous either: there are images of a love which builds a Hell in Heaven's despite – the fell hounds of Orsino's desire, the unmuzzled thoughts spoken of by Olivia. Such feelings intrude directly into the play for a short time in Act V, when Orsino threatens to kill the thing he loves. And though Sebastian's supposed treachery towards Antonio turns out to be one more delusion, there lingers an awareness that such things are possible. A surprising number of references to plague and corruption in the imagery of the play cast a deep shadow beyond its brilliance. There are reminders, too, of a time that can't be fleeted as they did in the golden world: the clock upbraids Olivia with the waste of time, and the priest measures time by the distance it carries him towards his grave. There is even something a little sepulchral about the free maids who weave their thread with bones, and the song they sing is a mournful one about love's cruelty, instead of that kindness of love which is celebrated in the play itself. By invoking the bounty of man and nature the revellers of the Christmas season tried to keep out the winter wind and man's ingratitude. They could not wholly forget them, and their presence is never quite forgotten in *Twelfth Night*.

*

The mood of *Twelfth Night* is so subtle and at the same time so unified that it comes as a surprise to the producer or to the careful reader to discover how many minor confusions and inconsistencies there are in the play's construction. The second scene, for example, raises expectations which are never satisfied. Viola's remarks about the Captain's reliable appearance are so pointed that we expect him to have a fairly influential part in the plot. But he fades out of the play at once. Shakespeare himself seems uneasy about his disappearance, because he suddenly informs us in the last scene that the Captain is detained on a charge brought against him by Malvolio. But this fresh evidence of Malvolio's ill will towards men is used only to bring him back himself on to the stage, and when he finally stalks off we are still – as Orsino exclaims – in the dark about the Captain. A further puzzle created by the second scene is that it leads us to expect Viola will sing to the Duke, but she never does so. Other mysterious features of the action are the unexplained substitution of Fabian for Feste in the trick played on Malvolio, and the sudden entrance in Act V of Sir Toby and Sir Andrew bleeding from a second encounter with Sebastian of which we have been told nothing. In the same scene, events which seem to have happened in a couple of days are said to have occupied three months. This kind of double time is so common in Shakespeare's plays that it is of no significance in itself, but here it does contribute to the general effect that *Twelfth Night*, for all its harmony of mood, is far from being a conventionally well-made play.

There are two ways of explaining these inconsistencies. One explanation is that the text of the play as we now have it represents a revision made some years after the first performance. Another is that the play was written at speed without having been thought out and planned in consistent detail. A test case for deciding, however tentatively, between these two views is offered by the scene that seems to bear the most obvious signs of revision, that between Viola and the Duke Orsino in the second Act. This starts with Orsino calling, in verse, for 'That old and antique song we heard last night'. He is told, in prose, that the singer is not present but can be found, and while Feste is fetched the tune is played and Orsino explains to Viola that the song is 'old and plain'. The song that Feste sings, however, is not a ballad or folk-song, but an up-to-date 'air'.

The explanation usually offered for all this is that, when the play was revived, perhaps about 1606, Feste had to be substituted for Viola as the singer because the voice of the boy who played Viola in the revival was breaking; and that Feste chose to sing a different song from the one Viola had sung in the original production. A similar theory has been used to explain the omission of the willow song in *Othello* as it was printed in 1622 – much more plausibly, for there we seem to have a genuine and rather obvious acting cut. But there are no awkwardnesses that suggest revision in Act II, scene 4 of *Twelfth Night*. The scene is a dramatic climax, perfectly conceived and perfectly executed. Viola, in her disguise as Cesario, is no longer the Duke Orsino's singer, but has been 'much advanced' to someone who summons others to sing for him – a sort of Master of the Duke's Music. Feste's entrance is delayed in order that background music may be used to stress the stagy melancholy of Orsino's love, and in order to draw the audience's attention to Viola's feelings for Orsino. Feste not only furnishes the song but also, by his slight asperity and mockery of Orsino, separates the Duke's more shallow feelings from the scene's final statement of Viola's double sorrow: her unspoken, hopeless love for Orsino and her grief for her missing brother.

Shakespeare in fact speaks 'masterly' in this scene, and it is hard to believe that the writing of it was not part of his original inspiration. If we are to call it a revised scene we need perhaps first to revise our own notions of what constitutes a revision. A playwright can revise his intentions while he is actually writing a play, and the practice of Brecht and other modern dramatists has shown how much further revision can go on in rehearsals, as the author improves on his script, or adapts it to the abilities of his actors. All such revisions will be incorporated into the acting copy, or promptbook, and precede the play's first performance. Other revisions may be carried out later by the playwright to meet the theatrical exigencies of a revival; it is fairly clear that 'God' was replaced by 'Jove' at several points in the text of *Twelfth Night* which has come down to us, in order to make the play conform with the 1606 statute against profanity in the theatre. Yet other changes in a play may be made years later and without the playwright's knowledge. Shakespeare's fellow actors presumably saw no harm in adding the odd topical joke to his plays from time to time. The mysterious allusion in Act II, scene 5 to the lady of the Strachy who married the yeoman of the wardrobe may well be a piece of Blackfriars gossip current after Shakespeare's death; perhaps it was slipped in for the Court performance of 1623.

But most of the other so-called revisions of *Twelfth Night* could be of the kind that precede the first performance. Shakespeare at first meant Viola to sing to Orsino, and tells us as much in the second scene; later, when he came to write Act II, scene 4, he realized that he could create an enthralling effect by having Viola sit listening beside her master, as moved as he by the music but able to give only indirect expression to her feelings. Having written this scene as it now stands, Shakespeare perhaps realized that Feste's part was becoming very heavy, and accordingly substituted Fabian for him in the plot against Malvolio. A sound dramatic instinct was also at work in this change of plan. The box-tree episode was Malvolio's big scene, and the Fool's popularity with the audience might have detracted from the effect Shakespeare was aiming at here. So the main encounter between Malvolio and Feste is deferred until the dark house scene in Act IV, in which Malvolio is heard but not seen and in which Feste can therefore be given full scope.

Shakespeare's admirers have often been reluctant to see in the inconsistencies of his texts the result of rapid *ad hoc* decisions by the playwright in the very course of composition. But a degree of improvisation is natural to drama; and the tradition that Shakespeare wrote *The Merry Wives of Windsor* in a fortnight at Queen Elizabeth's request, whether it is true or not, at least suggests that plays could be commissioned at very short notice. As a brilliant improvisation, *Twelfth Night* offers us the pleasure of tracing the artist's hand at work. It is no less an achievement for having been written at speed and perhaps for a special occasion.

The play's sprinkling of legal jokes suggests that this special occasion was the Middle Temple performance watched by Manningham on Candlemas night, 1602. But two arguments have been advanced for dating the play a year earlier than this. The first of these is based on two allusions, in the course of the dialogue, to the Shah of Persia. As the infatuated Malvolio, clutching Maria's letter and practising smiles, moves out of earshot of the plotters, Fabian (II.5.173–4) exclaims: 'I will not give my part of this sport for a pension of thousands to be paid from the Sophy.' Later on, Sir Andrew's fears of Cesario as a duelling opponent are doubled when he is told (III.4.272) that the youth 'has been fencer to the Sophy'. The Sophy or Shah of the time, Abbas the Great, was known about in England as the result of an expedition to Persia in 1599 led by two adventurers, Sir Anthony Shirley and his brother Sir Robert Shirley. The leaders of the expedition did not return to England. Sir Robert Shirley stayed in Persia, virtually as 'fencer to the Sophy', in order to reorganize the Persian army, while Sir Anthony, after receiving gifts which included sixteen thousand pistolets – 'a pension of thousands' – prevailed on the Shah to appoint him ambassador to the Christian Princes of Europe. But two other members of the expedition who did return to England published anonymously in the autumn of 1600 a small pamphlet called *The True Report of Sir Anthony Shirley's Journey*. It has been suggested that Shakespeare saw in this story of the expedition a way of drawing attention to the plight of the Shirleys' patron, the

Earl of Essex, whose life had been in jeopardy since his attempted palace revolution of the previous summer; and that the allusions to the Shah therefore fix the date of *Twelfth Night* as somewhere between the publication of *The True Report* and Essex's execution in February 1601.

There is nothing, however, in these two slight allusions to suggest that Shakespeare thought of the Shirley expedition as a diplomatic triumph. The government certainly did not see it in this light. They were thoroughly embarrassed by it, and quickly suppressed *The True Report.* A year later, however, Shakespeare could have heard a great deal about the Shirleys from his former close associate in the Lord Chamberlain's company of actors, Will Kemp, who in the late summer of 1601 returned from a continental tour which had included a meeting in Rome with Sir Anthony Shirley. Kemp's account of this, which was common talk at the time, together with a fuller account of the expedition published legitimately in September 1601, are the most likely sources for Shakespeare's two allusions to the Shah, and therefore support a date in the acting season 1601–1602 for *Twelfth Night.*

The second argument for the date 1600/1601 is based on the name of the play's leading male part. Orsino, Duke of Bracciano, was the name of a Florentine nobleman who visited England that winter and who was entertained by Queen Elizabeth on Twelfth Night – 6 January 1601 – with festivities that included the performance of a play in the Great Chamber of Whitehall Palace. In his memorandum of the many things to be done for the occasion, the Lord Chamberlain noted down that he had to confer with the Master of the Revels about the choice of a play 'that shall be best furnished with rich apparel, have great variety and change of music and dances, and of a subject that may be most pleasing to her majesty'. This memorandum, together with the title of the play and the name 'Orsino', have been taken as proof that *Twelfth Night* had its first night at Whitehall on 6 January 1601.

Queen Elizabeth's requirements would, however, have been better met by many other extant plays. *Twelfth Night* has no dances other than Sir Andrew's brief capers. Besides, only a threadbare inventiveness would give the title *Twelfth Night* to a play written for performance on the sixth of January. *A Midsummer Night's Dream* was not written for 24 June nor Chapman's *All Fools* for 1 April. All three titles indicate, not the date of performance, but a mood of licensed jesting. Finally, Shakespeare's choice of the name Orsino makes it virtually impossible for *Twelfth Night* to have been the play acted before the Duke of Bracciano. We only have to translate the episode into modern terms – a Royal Command performance on the occasion of a State Visit – to see how unthinkable it would be to use the important visitor's name for the chief character in a comedy. The rigid etiquette of Queen Elizabeth's court would have rendered such a joke impossible. On this very occasion a play by Ben Jonson which a company of child actors, the Children of the Revels, had hoped to perform before the Queen was rejected because – Jonson's modern editors argue – it contained a tactless reference to the disgrace of Essex. It is hard to believe that it would have been 'most pleasing to her majesty' to see her guest portrayed as Orsino or herself as Olivia.

If, though, Shakespeare was among the actors of an unidentified play performed by the Lord Chamberlain's Men in the Great Chamber on 6 January 1601, he must have been struck by the appearance of the guest of honour: the slight but splendid figure of the Duke Orsino as he stood by the Queen's side throughout the performance.

And when, a year later, he was called upon to write a festive comedy either for one of the three Christmas performances that his company gave at Court or for the Middle Temple feast in February, it would be natural for him to remember the name Orsino and to use it for his leading character. He may even have recalled the real Duke's reputation for hotheaded family pride when he came to write Act V, in which Orsino reacts so bitterly to the favour shown by Olivia towards his page Cesario.

A sign of Shakespeare's rapid writing in *Twelfth Night* is the freedom with which he borrows from his own work. When he was pressed for time it was inevitable that his thoughts should fly to incidents and characters which had gone down well with the audiences for his earlier comedies. Indeed there are so many self-borrowings in *Twelfth Night* that the play has been called 'a masterpiece of recapitulation'. The deeply loyal friend Antonio comes without so much as a change of name from *The Merchant of Venice*; Slender of *The Merry Wives of Windsor* brings his mincing oaths with him when he becomes Sir Andrew Aguecheek, and Shakespeare was counting on his fellow-shareholder in the company, Richard Cowley, to repeat his success in interpreting this 'silly ass' type of role. The comic possibilities of eavesdropping, explored in *Much Ado About Nothing*, and of girl disguised as boy, exploited in *As You Like It*, are stretched yet further in *Twelfth Night*, the one in the box-tree scene and the other in the duel.

Two situations in particular Shakespeare knew from experience to be ready sources of laughter. One was the arrival of a stranger in a town where he was immediately mistaken for his twin brother. As Manningham noticed, Shakespeare had already borrowed this unfailingly funny device from Plautus when writing *The Comedy of Errors* – a play which had entertained another Inn of Court at their feast eight years previously. Equally attractive was the Polly Oliver theme: the girl who follows her lover disguised as a page. Shakespeare had tried this out in *The Two Gentlemen of Verona*, a play which appears to have left him discontented since he kept trying to find new uses for its components. The inherent liveliness of the plot of *Twelfth Night* owes a great deal to the skill with which Shakespeare has combined these two comic situations. But he was not the first to combine them. A whole family group of plays and stories merging the twin situation with the Polly Oliver situation already existed by 1602, and Shakespeare certainly knew some of this group. If we follow Manningham's clue, we find among them two Italian plays called *Gl'Inganni* – the Deceptions – but these are less close to *Twelfth Night* than is an earlier play which was a source for both of them, *Gl'Ingannati* – the Deceived – acted at Siena in 1531.

Discussions of a literary source are often hard or tedious to follow because of the differences in names to be met with in two versions of the same plot. The use of generic names may help us to keep things clear here: the lover, for the character corresponding to Orsino; the brother, for Sebastian's counterpart; the lady, for Olivia's; and the heroine, for the character in Viola's situation. In *Gl'Ingannati*, the heroine assumes her disguise in order to follow and serve a lover who has apparently forgotten all about her during her temporary absence from Modena, the scene of the play, and who in fact now woos a lady to whom he sends the heroine as emissary. The lady promptly falls in love with the disguised heroine. Next the heroine's father and his friend, the ageing father of the lady (himself a suitor to the heroine) hear of her disguise, intercept her – or so they think – and shut her up with the lady. Actually they have seized the heroine's long-lost brother, who has just arrived in the city. On discovering what has occurred, the lover flies into a rage of jealousy and frustration; but he is brought to realize, through the eloquence of the heroine's old nurse, what a treasure he already has in the heroine's devotion.

This bald narration of its plot makes *Gl'Ingannati* sound very much as if it were the direct source of *Twelfth Night*. Actually the two plays are quite different in spirit. The Italian comedy has a realistic background of recent history. Its heroine was raped in the sack of Rome in 1527; in Modena she has had the good fortune to find a lover who belongs 'to the same political party' as herself. This is a long way from Shakespeare's Illyria; and in her heartless amusement at the lady's predicament, the heroine of *Gl'Ingannati* is a very long way from Viola. The whole play is in fact a heartless work; a bright, bustling, and often salacious comedy of intrigue. But it must have been very popular: French and Spanish translations soon appeared, and the plot was adapted for short stories by the Italian Bandello, the Frenchman Belleforest, and the Englishman Barnaby Rich. Each of these narrative versions carries us a little farther away from the harsh topicality of *Gl'Ingannati*, towards the Illyrian world represented in the sixteenth century by many translations of late Greek romances. Barnaby Rich's version, for example, which he called 'Apolonius and Silla', and published in 1581 as the second story in a volume entitled *Farewell to Military Profession* (he was a retired soldier), starts where many such romances start, with a shipwreck. This disaster brings the heroine to Constantinople, where she assumes her disguise in order to seek service with the lover, who is now raised to a dukedom and who, unlike the lover in the Italian versions of the tale, has not previously plighted his troth to the heroine. The lover sends the heroine to the lady, here a widow, and his messages are loyally delivered. Meanwhile the heroine's brother arrives in Constantinople and is entertained by the lady in mistake for the disguised heroine, with whom she has become infatuated. The brother shortly afterwards leaves. The lover now makes a direct approach to the lady, who tells him that she is promised to another. From servants' talk, the lover discovers that this rival is his own page. He immediately throws the heroine into prison. Next the lady discovers herself to be pregnant, and in desperation comes to the lover and tells him that his supposed page is the child's father. This compels the heroine to reveal that she is a girl. Overcome by gratitude for her devotion, the lover marries her; the lady's reputation is saved by the return of the brother and by their subsequent marriage.

For all its absurdity, this story is clearly closer to *Twelfth Night* than is any previous version. Several verbal echoes confirm Shakespeare's debt to Rich's story, which had the advantage of being in English and being easily available – another dramatist had made a play out of the first story in Rich's collection only a couple of years earlier. At the same time, Shakespeare knew and used some foreign versions of the tale. What happened may have been something like this. Asked for a comedy, Shakespeare recalled and almost certainly re-read Rich's 'Apolonius and Silla' because he liked its blend of two themes that he had already used with success. Then he must have remembered or discovered that there were in fact dramatic versions of this tale already extant. One, a Latin translation of *Gl'Ingannati*, had been acted at Cambridge before the Earl of Essex as recently as 1595, and Shakespeare could have borrowed a manuscript of this from his Stratford acquaintance and future son-in-law John Hall, who had been at Cambridge at the time. Or he could have glanced through a copy of the original Italian play; or come across the close translation of it into French, which had the distinction of being the first prose comedy in that language. He certainly knew *Gl'Ingannati* in the original or translation, since some details in *Twelfth Night* derive from no other source: the brother's sightseeing in the city, the heroine's hopeless passion described as though (II.4.106) it were experienced by someone else –

My father had a daughter loved a man . . .

– and the servant's invitation to the brother, whom he mistakes for the disguised heroine, to come and visit the lady. Moreover, Shakespeare was familiar with the tale in the collections of Bandello and Belleforest. Not only are their re-tellings echoed verbally several times in *Twelfth Night*, but both writers place the emotional climax of the story in the heroine's attempt to dissuade the lover from his pursuit of the lady; and we have already seen that the episode in *Twelfth Night* which corresponds to this, Act II, scene 4, is a highlight of the play. It has no counterpart in Rich's story.

All these recollections did not prevent Shakespeare from handling the tale in his own way. His Viola does not assume her disguise in pursuit of the man she loves; she falls in love with Orsino only after she has found service with him. Olivia is not a widow (her mourning must have misled Manningham) but a young girl who repels the Duke Orsino's suit because she is stricken with grief for her brother's death. Viola too loves a brother she believes to be dead; and the brother himself is not brought in merely to complicate the plot and then disappear, but is a positive and likeable character whose impetuous marriage to Olivia establishes, in a world of fantasies, one irrefutable fact from which the dénouement can be swiftly and gaily reached. All these changes help to normalize and humanize Rich's melodramatic tale. However many versions of the story may have been known to Shakespeare, he succeeded in shaping it afresh with deftness and confidence.

What Rich calls 'a leash of lovers' derives, then, from 'Apolonius and Silla' and from some of the tales and plays that preceded it. But there are no hints in these earlier versions of Antonio, nor of Malvolio and his tormentors. Yet for Manningham, the memorable scenes were those in which Malvolio figured, and his response was typical of its time. When the play was acted at Court in 1623, it was called *Malvolio*, and Charles I changed the title to this in his own copy of the second edition of Shakespeare's works.

A suggestion for the baiting of Malvolio could have come from Rich's book. One of his tales is about a man who married a scold. Driven to desperation by her clamour, he shut her up

> *in a dark house that was on his back side; and then, calling his neighbours about her, he would seem with great sorrow to lament his wife's distress, telling them that she was suddenly become lunatic; whereas, by his gesture, he took so great grief as though he would likewise have run mad for company. But his wife (as he had attired her) seemed indeed not to be well in her wits but, seeing her husband's manners, showed herself in her conditions to be a right Bedlam. She used no other words but curses and bannings, crying for the plague and the pestilence, and that the devil would tear her husband in pieces. The company that were about her, they would exhort her, 'Good neighbour, forget these speeches which doth so much distemper you, and call upon God, and he will surely help you.'*

In just the same way, Feste exhorts Malvolio to leave his

vain bibble-babble and Maria bids him remember his prayers. But if this passage gave Shakespeare his first idea for the trick played on Malvolio, Malvolio himself quickly grew far beyond the stature of a mere dupe in his creator's mind. In fact he is so sharply particularized that there is a strong likelihood that when he appeared 'in the habit of some sir of note' he was recognized as the caricature of some unpopular figure of the time, well known to a Court, or Middle Temple, audience. Malvolio's alleged Puritanism, his dislike of bear-baiting, his 'august regard of control', and his interruption of a noisy revel, have all been taken to point to Sir William Knollys, the Controller of the Queen's Household. Even the name Malvolio has been read as a reference to Knollys's notorious infatuation with his ward Mary Fitton ('I-want-Mall'), whose disgrace at Court in the winter of 1600–1601 may be alluded to when Sir Toby speaks of the picture of Mistress Mall which has taken dust.

Whether or not this and other identifications of characters in *Twelfth Night* with real people are correct, they help to remind us of one aspect of the play which stage designers, eager to hoist sail for the Mediterranean, too easily overlook: its Englishness. Shakespeare's Illyria is within hailing distance of the Thames watermen, and the visitor from Messaline puts up in the south suburbs, at the Elephant – as did many other visitors to London. Shakespeare had learned a good deal about the possibilities of realistic social comedy when he had acted in Ben Jonson's *Every Man in His Humour* some three years before *Twelfth Night* was written. The oddities of Jonson's Stephano were still vivid in Shakespeare's memory when he invented the part of Sir Andrew Aguecheek. Both are typical English country 'gulls' – the Elizabethan word for anyone easily taken in – both echo the phrases of more inventive characters, both demean themselves by abusing their social inferiors, both waver between bluster and timidity, both are convinced they have a very pretty leg worth clothing in fine hose. Yet to speak of *Every Man in His Humour* as a 'source' for *Twelfth Night* is to be reminded once more of Shakespeare's skill in subjugating all the elements that go to make up the play to its dominant mood of festivity. Stephano is an object of real contempt to Jonson; but such is the spirit of *Twelfth Night* that Shakespeare, a bad hater at all times, enjoys his Sir Andrew and endears him to us as somebody who 'was adored once, too'.

*

This introduction has been more concerned with the mood and atmosphere of *Twelfth Night* than with an interpretation of its characters. Actors and producers must of course give much thought to such interpretations, but these are necessarily conditioned by their grasp of the play's own character. Moreover, their readings of characters in the play are bound to be still further modified by the way the actors' abilities interact in the company as a whole. For example, a sympathetic, or simply pathetic, Sir Andrew presupposes a Sir Toby whose dark, rascally side must be exposed to the audience long before his final repudiation of his fellow-knight. Contrast in itself is not enough; a tomboyish Viola, who enjoys scrapping with Olivia's attendants, does not sort well with a mournfully infatuated Olivia. In fact an almost operatic principle of contrast is too often seen at work in the play's casting, and this is especially true of the age of the characters. Sixty years ago, Orsino was a part for the greying matinée idol, and even Harley Granville-Barker, who did so much to free Shakespeare production from its nineteenth-century conventions, spoke of him as 'your middle-aged romantic'. True, Olivia thinks Orsino no match for her in years, but at eighteen or so – and Olivia should be no more – five or six years constitute a great gap. Elsewhere she speaks of his 'fresh and stainless youth', and this accords with the way the lover is presented in earlier versions of the tale. Bandello describes him as not yet twenty.

The trend in productions at the present is away from a straight to a satiric playing of Orsino. Unfortunately in the process he has sometimes been transformed into what one critic calls the Moony Duke. A little absurd he must be; but his absurdity can well consist in his eagerness, the zest with which he plays the role of the romantic lover. He is like Romeo before he has met Juliet and while he still fancies himself in love with Rosalind: changeful and moody, his mind a very opal. Just as Romeo forgets he can feed off his love and starts asking about dinner, so Orsino forgets his generalization that men's fancies are more giddy and infirm than women's are; five minutes later, he is insisting that there is no comparison between the love a woman can bear him and that he owes Olivia. Yet this absurdity must never submerge what is genuinely 'romantic' in the role, the appeal, as C. S. Lewis has described it, of a foreign duke 'speaking golden syllables, wearing rich clothes, and standing in the centre of the stage'.

Olivia for her part is too often played as – in the words of a modern producer – 'the stately contralto whom a sudden bereavement has distracted from the organization of the Hunt Ball'. Shakespeare deliberately turned the widow he found in his chief source into a young girl; perhaps a young girl rather like Queen Victoria at her accession, awed by her responsibilities and determined to be good. She can be prim, circumspect, shyly severe with the extraordinary household left at her command. She wants to do the right thing, and is appalled when she finds the fair young man at the gate has been intercepted by Sir Toby, a most embarrassing relation to have about the house. Then, when the fair young man appears, we watch the awakening of the Sleeping Beauty, from her firm denial (I.5.246) – 'I cannot love him' – to lively, responsive repartee, then (guided by Shakespeare's internal stage direction) to her speaking in starts, distractedly, and so finally to the admission that she, hitherto so self-possessed, has caught the plague: 'ourselves we do not owe'. Her big scene with Viola in Act III gives the actress a splendid chance to show the audience how Olivia has grown up. It is important to control the comedy of this scene, so that Olivia does not appear ludicrous because she is in love, but only because she has fallen in love with a girl disguised as a boy. Her frankness in love should be as attractive as Juliet's, and make her the embodiment of a festive generosity. Her love is madness only in its lack of a true object; as soon as Viola is replaced by Sebastian it becomes reasonable love as that is defined by Barnaby Rich in 'Apolonius and Silla': 'If a question might be asked, "What is the ground indeed of reasonable love, whereby the knot is knit of true and perfect friendship?" I think those that be wise would answer, "Desert"; that is, where the party beloved doth requite us with the like.'

The actress who takes on the part of Viola also has to resist the temptation to play for the wrong kind of laughs. The Victorians, who gave us the Principal Boy, expected their actresses to make fun of the equivocations of Viola's disguise. The first producer to rebel against the nineteenth-century style of acting this part was Harley Granville-Barker, whose Savoy Theatre production of 1912 was perhaps the most famous *Twelfth Night* in theatrical history. Granville-Barker's knowledge of Elizabethan stage conditions made him sharply aware of the anachronism of a swaggering and gruff-toned actress in the part. When the Viola of 1602 disguised as Cesario, the boy-actor retained his natural gait and his 'maiden pipe'. The part itself has demands enough, without an additional obligation on the player to slip in and out of the Cesario manner. For example, at the end of Act II, scene 4, Viola's words

> *I am all the daughters of my father's house,*
> *And all the brothers too*

must deepen the melancholy of the scene by adding to her helpless love for Orsino her hopeless grief for her brother. It is catastrophic if, in order to get an easy laugh, the actress at this point gives a start and seems to correct herself in the phrase 'And all the brothers too'. Again there have been Violas who, in the willow-cabin speech in Act I, scene 5, have deliberately stumbled over 'Olivia!' as if they had been on the point of saying 'Orsino!' But Viola's great virtue is the generosity which makes her sink her own feelings in Orsino's, so that here she speaks entirely in her master's voice; any hesitation destroys the moving effect of this utter self-forgetfulness.

Sebastian's role is perhaps more of a problem for the producer than it is for the actor. Stage twins are never easy to cast. One unfortunate Sebastian between the wars had to look like two different Violas at successive performances as two famous actresses alternated in the chief female parts. It is not really surprising that some producers have tried to dispense with Sebastian altogether. Nevertheless, it is shocking. The reunion of brother and sister cannot be left to ventriloquism or to a trick with mirrors. It is the dramatic climax of the play's last Act, and completes its celebration of generous love, by adding the feelings of those whose ties are of blood to the feelings of the friends and of the lovers. Any dissimilarity there may be between the twins goes unnoticed at this point, because Shakespeare quickly diverts our attention from the bystanders' astonishment over this 'natural perspective', and focuses it instead on the exquisitely conveyed emotions of the brother and sister, as they hesitate before the great sea of joys which threatens to overwhelm them. Sebastian must be played as someone who can inspire such feelings in his sister and in his friend, and who will be a worthy husband for the Countess Olivia. He matters very much, that is to say, in the play's total effect. His part is short and relatively simple, but it is a strong one.

If stage interpretations of the lovers in *Twelfth Night* have changed little since Victorian times, the playing of Malvolio has, in some recent productions, been strongly influenced by a twentieth-century sociological reading of the play. According to such a reading, *Twelfth Night* depicts an Elizabethan household in transition from the easy-going paternalism that always kept a place by the fire for people like Feste and Sir Toby, to a new economic order of things dominated by the efficient, utterly uncharitable Malvolio. As an overall interpretation of the play, this view has one serious flaw. *Twelfth Night* is not about Olivia's household. Like every version of the story from *Gl'Ingannati* onwards, it is about Viola and her predicament, and any interpretation that moves Viola from the centre to the periphery of the play's interest is bound to make us cry out: 'I care not for your play of good life: give me a love play.' But this sociological approach has its appeal for actors used to playing Shaw, and modern productions often give Olivia a diligent, self-made steward, socially angular perhaps, but thoroughly responsible; every office and school staff-room contains such a Malvolio. This interpretation is full of hazards and difficulties, in spite of its superficial appeal. The differences between Malvolio and his social betters were plain to the play's first audience: yellow stockings, cross-gartered, were comically unfashionable by 1602, as was Malvolio's use of words like 'element', which the courtly jester Feste knows to be 'overworn'. But how can it be conveyed to a modern audience, on whom these distinctions are wasted, that Malvolio comes from a class that has lagged behind the fashionable world? Actors who try to get the point across by dropped aitches are guilty of an anachronism as well as a gross vulgarization. And a further danger in this class-conscious presentation of Malvolio is that it makes him much too sympathetic. We live in the world of responsible executives, and if Malvolio is presented to us as one of them the tricks played on him appear cruel and unjustified – the spite of the old and impoverished gentry against the class who were, in the revolution of 1642, to be 'revenged on the whole pack' of them.

The festive mood of the play is much better preserved if Malvolio is presented to us as a psychological rather than a social misfit. He is incapable of the easy give and take of those who are 'generous, guiltless, and of free disposition'. Most of the great stage Malvolios have been stiff as ramrods, and the play's best laughs come from the unexpected rapidity with which the ramrod unbends. There is comic justice in the process; Malvolio, who refuses to acknowledge that there is a time to dance, that people sometimes need cakes and ale, is tricked into the most outrageously untimely skittishness and facetiousness. Act III, scene 4 needs to be played as a transformation scene, perhaps even with Malvolio breaking into song; 'Please one and please all' was, after all, an Elizabethan pop song, though unfortunately the music has not survived. Next there is thrust upon him, by Maria's letter, the further role of being distant with Sir Toby, which produces a delicious exaggeration of his usual manner. What makes this most admirable fooling is that it is completely integrated with the play's main theme. Malvolio hates to give himself away. He won't play spontaneously; but with gain in view – the prospect of being Count Malvolio – he eagerly makes a fool of himself.

A sociological reading of the play has also left its mark on the behaviour of the plotters in the device against Malvolio. On the whole, this has had the good effect of toning down the traditional slapstick playing of these scenes. Maria must of course be small and shrill and the sort of young woman who finds life intensely dramatic. But she is not a hoyden, and the part will probably be played as the kind of waiting-gentlewoman Shakespeare had in mind if the actress conceives of her as a poor relation with no dowry, anxious to find a husband before she is relegated to the shelf. Sir Toby too is often presented nowadays as a character who, it is said, could gain admission to, and be helped out of, the best clubs in London. In fact the reaction against playing some scenes of the play as sheer farce has now gone rather far. There has even been a production without a box-tree, presumably because of some notion of Shakespeare's bare stage. But the Elizabethan public theatre made use of very solid properties, including trees; and it is a pity to deny any audience the fun of watching faces – aghast, apoplectic, or delighted – appear through the foliage. By and large, however, the new restraint has had the welcome effect of restoring the play's balance and its unity of mood, so that the drinking and devising scenes become comic relief in the sense that they heighten the comic effect, and not in the sense that they offer relaxation from more serious matters. For all the characters in the play, with two exceptions, are to some degree absurd. Olivia, by her own admission, is as mad as Malvolio, and Fortune plays some ludicrous tricks on the twins.

The two exceptions are Feste and Antonio. As a character Feste must have owed much to the genius – for one feels it was just that – of Robert Armin, who joined Shakespeare's company when it moved to The Globe Theatre in 1599, and whose creations included Touchstone and the Fool in *King Lear* as well as Feste. Armin played a 'sage fool' or professional jester, whose business was to mock the pedantry of the learned, bandy words skilfully with the witty, moralize on the vanity of womankind, and entertain everyone by his songs. In keeping with this concept, Feste is the source of much of the play's laughter; but he is not, unlike earlier Shakespeare clowns, its object. Indeed many actors have been tempted into playing him as a kind of Pagliacci, half concealing a breaking heart beneath the motley. But though Feste is, as we have seen, a character who from time to time steps out of the play's festive atmosphere, it is his detachment, and not a passionate attachment to Olivia or anyone else, that gives him his special and moving place in the play. Harley Granville-Barker ended his Savoy Theatre production by having the huge golden gates of Olivia's house slowly close on the rejoicing couples, leaving Feste outside to sing plaintively about the wind and the rain. It is perhaps even more effective if Feste sings this song about the ages of man with a certain briskness. Throughout the play Feste has stressed the need to use time wisely; since 'there is a time to everything under the sun', he knows that in the passing of life he now sings about his fooling grows old too. The depth and strength of Feste's character lies not in any tragic dimension, nor even in that pathos which is the invention of Romantic and post-Romantic criticism, but in its solid basis of stoical common sense.

If there is any hint of tragedy in a play written a year or two after *Hamlet*, it is to be found in Antonio rather than in Feste. Antonio's protestation of his love for Sebastian, and his bitter outcry at his supposed betrayal, are the true voice of feeling. They stir us painfully, even though we know all will come right in the end, because they move outside comedy's range of emotions in a way that Orsino's melodramatic outburst in Act V does not. And when the play ends, Antonio, like his namesake in *The Merchant of Venice*, is odd man out. He has regained his faith in his friend, but that friend can pay little attention to him in the excitement of finding himself restored to Viola and married to Olivia. Although Antonio is inside the golden gate, he does not belong to the golden world. Producers seem uneasily aware of this isolation, and dress him up as a stage pirate in a desperate attempt to make him part of the Illyrian scene. But if Shakespeare has given us in this character a fragment of personal experience – the experience which is expressed in numerous sonnets and which makes betrayal of trust a dominant theme of his tragedies – we must accept this as a rare revelation. One day a producer may be bold enough to free Antonio from his pirate disguise and instead make him up to look like the Droeshout engraving of Shakespeare himself. To do this would be wholly in the spirit of a play which evokes, and makes us free citizens of, a world of mirth, and yet at the same time keeps us aware of a world where malice is seldom 'sportful', nor time golden.

FURTHER READING

(1) *Editions*

The best fully-annotated edition of *Twelfth Night* is that by J. M. Lothian and T. W. Craik in the new Arden series (1975). A paperback reprint is available of the fifth edition (1901) of Horace Howard Furness's presentation of the play in the New Variorum Shakespeare; it reproduces the Folio text of the play together with a wealth of eighteenth- and nineteenth-century comments. Sidney Musgrove has produced an 'old-spelling' edition for the general reader (1969).

(2) *Background Material*

Rich's 'Apolonius and Silla' is given in full in *Elizabethan Love Stories*, edited by T. J. B. Spencer (Penguin Shakespeare Library, 1968), as well as in the Variorum edition of *Twelfth Night*, which includes some other source material. An indispensable work on the sources of *Twelfth Night* is volume 2 (*The Comedies, 1597–1603*) of *Narrative and Dramatic Sources of Shakespeare* (1957–), edited by Geoffrey Bullough. This has a lively translation of *Gl'Ingannati* and a full discussion of the many suggested sources of Shakespeare's play. Other discussions are to be found in Kenneth Muir's *Shakespeare's Sources*, volume 1, *Comedies and Tragedies* (1957), and in an article by René Pruvost with the title '*The Two Gentlemen of Verona, Twelfth Night* et *Gl'Ingannati*' which appeared in volume 13 of *Études Anglaises* (1960).

Two views of the play's origins which are briefly discussed in the Introduction are represented by Leslie Hotson's *The First Night of Twelfth Night* (1954, paperback 1961) and John W. Draper's *The Twelfth Night of Shakespeare's Audience* (1950). The first of these is questioned in 'Topicality and the Date of

Twelfth Night' by Josephine W. Bennett in the *South Atlantic Quarterly*, volume 71 (1972), and the second is challenged in 'The *Twelfth Night* of Shakespeare and of Professor Draper' by N. A. Brittain in *Shakespeare Quarterly*, volume 7 (1956).

(3) *Criticism*

Recent general works on Shakespeare's comedies which form a good background to *Twelfth Night* are: John Russell Brown's *Shakespeare and his Comedies* (1957); C. L. Barber's *Shakespeare's Festive Comedy* (Princeton, 1959); Northrop Frye's *A Natural Perspective* (New York, 1965); and the article 'The Mature Comedies' by Frank Kermode in *Early Shakespeare: Stratford-upon-Avon Studies*, 3, edited by J. R. Brown and B. Harris (1961). Special studies of the play include the articles of L. G. Salingar, 'The Design of *Twelfth Night*', *Shakespeare Quarterly*, volume 9 (1958), Joseph Summers, 'The Masks of *Twelfth Night*' in *Shakespeare: Modern Essays in Criticism* edited by L. F. Dean (New York, 1957), John Russell Brown's 'Directions for *Twelfth Night*' in *Shakespeare's Comedies: An Anthology of Criticism* edited by Laurence Lerner (Penguin Books, 1967), the same writer's admirable close reading of some passages from *Twelfth Night* in *Shakespeare's Dramatic Style* (1970), Terence Eagleton's 'Language and Reality in *Twelfth Night*' in *Critical Quarterly*, volume 9 (1967), and a book by Clifford Leech, *Twelfth Night and Shakespearean Comedy* (Toronto, 1965). Walter N. King has made a collection of *Twentieth Century Interpretations of Twelfth Night* (1968), and D. J. Palmer has compiled '*Twelfth Night*': *A Casebook* (1972). Three good articles published since these anthologies were made are: Alexander Leggatt's 'Shakespeare and the Borderlines of Comedy' in *Mosaic*, volume 5 (1971); Joan Hartwig's 'Feste's Whirligig and the Comic Providence of *Twelfth Night*' in the *Journal of English Literary History*, volume 40 (1973); Anne Barton's '*As You Like It* and *Twelfth Night*: Shakespeare's Sense of an Ending' in *Shakespearian Comedy: Stratford-upon-Avon Studies*, 14, edited by D. J. Palmer and M. Bradbury (1974).

FURTHER READING

The editors of the new Arden edition give a full account of the play's stage history. Arthur Colby Sprague and J. C. Trewin, in *Shakespeare's Plays Today* (1971), discuss changing theatrical interpretations of the play's roles, while the minor parts are analysed by Dennis R. Preston in *Shakespeare Quarterly*, volume 21 (1969). Feste has always aroused critical interest and scholarly inquiry. Our understanding of him is helped by Andrew Bradley's 'Feste the Jester' in *A Miscellany* (1929), Enid Welsford's *The Fool* (Cambridge, 1935), Leslie Hotson's *Shakespeare's Motley* (1952), R. H. Goldsmith's *Wise Fools in Shakespeare* (Liverpool, 1955), and Charles S. Felver's *Robert Armin* (New York, 1961). Harley Granville-Barker's Preface to his acting edition of the play has been reprinted in *Prefaces to Shakespeare*, volume 6 (1974). There is a chapter on the play's music in J. H. Long's *Shakespeare's Use of Music* (Florida, 1955) and a chapter on 'Adult Songs and Robert Armin' in *Music in Shakespearean Tragedy* (1963) by F. W. Sternfeld.

Finally, readers who disagree with my Introduction will enjoy F. H. Langman's onslaught in 'Comedy and Saturnalia: the Case of *Twelfth Night*', *Southern Review* (Adelaide), volume 7 (1974).

TWELFTH NIGHT

OR

WHAT YOU WILL

THE CHARACTERS IN THE PLAY

ORSINO, Duke of Illyria
VALENTINE } gentlemen attending on Orsino
CURIO }
First Officer
Second Officer

VIOLA, a shipwrecked lady, later disguised as Cesario
SEBASTIAN, her twin brother
CAPTAIN of the wrecked ship
ANTONIO, another sea-captain

OLIVIA, a countess
MARIA, her waiting-gentlewoman
SIR TOBY BELCH, her uncle
SIR ANDREW AGUECHEEK, Sir Toby's protégé
MALVOLIO, Olivia's steward
FABIAN, a member of her household
FESTE, her jester
A PRIEST
A SERVANT

Musicians, lords, sailors, attendants

Music. Enter Orsino Duke of Illyria, Curio, and other lords **I.1**

ORSINO

If music be the food of love, play on,
Give me excess of it, that, surfeiting,
The appetite may sicken, and so die.
That strain again! It had a dying fall.
O, it came o'er my ear like the sweet sound
That breathes upon a bank of violets,
Stealing and giving odour. Enough, no more!
'Tis not so sweet now as it was before.
O spirit of love, how quick and fresh art thou,
That, notwithstanding thy capacity 10
Receiveth as the sea, naught enters there,
Of what validity and pitch soe'er,
But falls into abatement and low price
Even in a minute. So full of shapes is fancy
That it alone is high fantastical.

CURIO

Will you go hunt, my lord?

ORSINO

What, Curio?

CURIO

The hart.

ORSINO

Why, so I do, the noblest that I have.
O, when mine eyes did see Olivia first, 20
Methought she purged the air of pestilence.

That instant was I turned into a hart,
And my desires, like fell and cruel hounds,
E'er since pursue me.

Enter Valentine

How now! What news from her?

VALENTINE

So please my lord, I might not be admitted,
But from her handmaid do return this answer:
The element itself, till seven years' heat,
Shall not behold her face at ample view,
But like a cloistress she will veilèd walk,
30 And water once a day her chamber round
With eye-offending brine; all this to season
A brother's dead love, which she would keep fresh
And lasting, in her sad remembrance.

ORSINO

O, she that hath a heart of that fine frame
To pay this debt of love but to a brother –
How will she love, when the rich golden shaft
Hath killed the flock of all affections else
That live in her; when liver, brain, and heart,
These sovereign thrones, are all supplied and filled –
40 Her sweet perfections – with one self king!
Away before me to sweet beds of flowers!
Love thoughts lie rich when canopied with bowers.

Exeunt

I.2 *Enter Viola, a Captain, and sailors*

VIOLA

What country, friends, is this?

CAPTAIN

This is Illyria, lady.

VIOLA

And what should I do in Illyria?

My brother, he is in Elysium.
Perchance he is not drowned. What think you, sailors?

CAPTAIN
It is perchance that you yourself were saved.

VIOLA
O, my poor brother! and so perchance may he be.

CAPTAIN
True, madam, and to comfort you with chance,
Assure yourself, after our ship did split,
When you and those poor number saved with you 10
Hung on our driving boat, I saw your brother,
Most provident in peril, bind himself –
Courage and hope both teaching him the practice –
To a strong mast, that lived upon the sea;
Where, like Arion on the dolphin's back,
I saw him hold acquaintance with the waves
So long as I could see.

VIOLA
For saying so, there's gold.
Mine own escape unfoldeth to my hope,
Whereto thy speech serves for authority, 20
The like of him. Knowest thou this country?

CAPTAIN
Ay, madam, well, for I was bred and born
Not three hours' travel from this very place.

VIOLA
Who governs here?

CAPTAIN
A noble Duke, in nature as in name.

VIOLA
What is his name?

CAPTAIN
Orsino.

VIOLA
Orsino . . . I have heard my father name him.

He was a bachelor then.

CAPTAIN

30 And so is now, or was so, very late;
For but a month ago I went from hence,
And then 'twas fresh in murmur – as you know,
What great ones do, the less will prattle of –
That he did seek the love of fair Olivia.

VIOLA

What's she?

CAPTAIN

A virtuous maid, the daughter of a count
That died some twelvemonth since, then leaving her
In the protection of his son, her brother,
Who shortly also died; for whose dear love,
40 They say, she hath abjured the sight
And company of men.

VIOLA

O, that I served that lady,
And might not be delivered to the world –
Till I had made mine own occasion mellow –
What my estate is.

CAPTAIN That were hard to compass,
Because she will admit no kind of suit,
No, not the Duke's.

VIOLA

There is a fair behaviour in thee, Captain,
And though that nature with a beauteous wall
50 Doth oft close in pollution, yet of thee
I will believe thou hast a mind that suits
With this thy fair and outward character.
I prithee – and I'll pay thee bounteously –
Conceal me what I am, and be my aid
For such disguise as haply shall become
The form of my intent. I'll serve this Duke.

Thou shalt present me as an eunuch to him.
It may be worth thy pains, for I can sing
And speak to him in many sorts of music
That will allow me very worth his service. 60
What else may hap to time I will commit.
Only shape thou thy silence to my wit.

CAPTAIN
Be you his eunuch, and your mute I'll be.
When my tongue blabs, then let mine eyes not see.

VIOLA
I thank thee. Lead me on. *Exeunt*

Enter Sir Toby Belch and Maria I.3

SIR TOBY What a plague means my niece to take the death of her brother thus? I am sure care's an enemy to life.

MARIA By my troth, Sir Toby, you must come in earlier o'nights. Your cousin, my lady, takes great exceptions to your ill hours.

SIR TOBY Why, let her except before excepted.

MARIA Ay, but you must confine yourself within the modest limits of order.

SIR TOBY Confine! I'll confine myself no finer than I am. These clothes are good enough to drink in, and so be 10 these boots too; an they be not, let them hang themselves in their own straps.

MARIA That quaffing and drinking will undo you. I heard my lady talk of it yesterday, and of a foolish knight that you brought in one night here, to be her wooer.

SIR TOBY Who? Sir Andrew Aguecheek?

MARIA Ay, he.

SIR TOBY He's as tall a man as any's in Illyria.

MARIA What's that to the purpose?

SIR TOBY Why, he has three thousand ducats a year. 20

MARIA Ay, but he'll have but a year in all these ducats. He's a very fool and a prodigal.

SIR TOBY Fie, that you'll say so. He plays o'the viol-de-gamboys, and speaks three or four languages word for word without book, and hath all the good gifts of nature.

MARIA He hath indeed all, most natural; for besides that he's a fool, he's a great quarreller; and but that he hath the gift of a coward to allay the gust he hath in quarrelling, 'tis thought among the prudent he would quickly have the gift of a grave.

SIR TOBY By this hand, they are scoundrels and substractors that say so of him. Who are they?

MARIA They that add, moreover, he's drunk nightly in your company.

SIR TOBY With drinking healths to my niece. I'll drink to her as long as there is a passage in my throat and drink in Illyria. He's a coward and a coistrel that will not drink to my niece till his brains turn o'the toe, like a parish top. What, wench! Castiliano, *vulgo* – for here comes Sir Andrew Agueface!

Enter Sir Andrew Aguecheek

SIR ANDREW Sir Toby Belch! How now, Sir Toby Belch?

SIR TOBY Sweet Sir Andrew!

SIR ANDREW Bless you, fair shrew.

MARIA And you too, sir.

SIR TOBY Accost, Sir Andrew, accost.

SIR ANDREW What's that?

SIR TOBY My niece's chambermaid.

SIR ANDREW Good Mistress Accost, I desire better acquaintance.

MARIA My name is Mary, sir.

SIR ANDREW Good Mistress Mary Accost –

SIR TOBY (*aside*) You mistake, knight. 'Accost' is front

her, board her, woo her, assail her.

SIR ANDREW (*aside*) By my troth, I would not undertake
her in this company. Is that the meaning of 'accost'?

MARIA Fare you well, gentlemen.

SIR TOBY (*aside*) An thou let part so, Sir Andrew, would
thou mightst never draw sword again.

SIR ANDREW An you part so, mistress, I would I might 60
never draw sword again. Fair lady, do you think you
have fools in hand?

MARIA Sir, I have not you by the hand.

SIR ANDREW Marry, but you shall have, and here's my
hand.

MARIA Now, sir, 'Thought is free.' I pray you, bring your
hand to the buttery bar and let it drink.

SIR ANDREW Wherefore, sweetheart? What's your metaphor?

MARIA It's dry, sir. 70

SIR ANDREW Why, I think so. I am not such an ass, but
I can keep my hand dry. But what's your jest?

MARIA A dry jest, sir.

SIR ANDREW Are you full of them?

MARIA Ay, sir. I have them at my fingers' ends. Marry,
now I let go your hand, I am barren. *Exit*

SIR TOBY O knight, thou lack'st a cup of canary. When
did I see thee so put down?

SIR ANDREW Never in your life, I think, unless you see
canary put me down. Methinks sometimes I have no 80
more wit than a Christian or an ordinary man has; but I
am a great eater of beef, and I believe that does harm to
my wit.

SIR TOBY No question.

SIR ANDREW An I thought that, I'd forswear it. I'll ride
home tomorrow, Sir Toby.

SIR TOBY *Pourquoi*, my dear knight?

SIR ANDREW What is *pourquoi*? Do or not do? I would I had bestowed that time in the tongues that I have in
90 fencing, dancing, and bear-baiting. O, had I but followed the arts!

SIR TOBY Then hadst thou had an excellent head of hair.

SIR ANDREW Why, would that have mended my hair?

SIR TOBY Past question, for thou seest it will not curl by nature.

SIR ANDREW But it becomes me well enough, does't not?

SIR TOBY Excellent, it hangs like flax on a distaff; and I hope to see a huswife take thee between her legs and spin it off.

100 SIR ANDREW Faith, I'll home tomorrow, Sir Toby. Your niece will not be seen, or if she be, it's four to one she'll none of me; the Count himself, here hard by, woos her.

SIR TOBY She'll none o'the Count; she'll not match above her degree, neither in estate, years, nor wit. I have heard her swear't. Tut, there's life in't, man.

SIR ANDREW I'll stay a month longer. I am a fellow o'the strangest mind i'the world. I delight in masques and revels sometimes altogether.

SIR TOBY Art thou good at these kickshawses, knight?

110 SIR ANDREW As any man in Illyria, whatsoever he be, under the degree of my betters, and yet I will not compare with an old man.

SIR TOBY What is thy excellence in a galliard, knight?

SIR ANDREW Faith, I can cut a caper.

SIR TOBY And I can cut the mutton to't.

SIR ANDREW And I think I have the back-trick, simply as strong as any man in Illyria.

SIR TOBY Wherefore are these things hid? Wherefore have these gifts a curtain before 'em? Are they like to
120 take dust, like Mistress Mall's picture? Why dost thou not go to church in a galliard and come home in a

coranto? My very walk should be a jig. I would not so much as make water but in a sink-apace. What dost thou mean? Is it a world to hide virtues in? I did think by the excellent constitution of thy leg it was formed under the star of a galliard.

SIR ANDREW Ay, 'tis strong, and it does indifferent well in a dun-coloured stock. Shall we set about some revels?

SIR TOBY What shall we do else? Were we not born under Taurus? 130

SIR ANDREW Taurus? That's sides and heart.

SIR TOBY No, sir, it is legs and thighs. Let me see thee caper. Ha! Higher! Ha! Ha! Excellent! *Exeunt*

Enter Valentine, and Viola in man's attire I.4

VALENTINE If the Duke continue these favours towards you, Cesario, you are like to be much advanced. He hath known you but three days, and already you are no stranger.

VIOLA You either fear his humour or my negligence, that you call in question the continuance of his love. Is he inconstant, sir, in his favours?

VALENTINE No, believe me.

Enter Orsino, Curio, and attendants

VIOLA I thank you. Here comes the Count.

ORSINO Who saw Cesario, ho? 10

VIOLA On your attendance, my lord, here.

ORSINO (*to Curio and attendants*)
Stand you awhile aloof. *(To Viola)* Cesario,
Thou knowest no less but all. I have unclasped
To thee the book even of my secret soul.
Therefore, good youth, address thy gait unto her.
Be not denied access; stand at her doors,
And tell them, there thy fixèd foot shall grow

Till thou have audience.

VIOLA Sure, my noble lord,
If she be so abandoned to her sorrow
20 As it is spoke, she never will admit me.

ORSINO
Be clamorous and leap all civil bounds
Rather than make unprofited return.

VIOLA
Say I do speak with her, my lord, what then?

ORSINO
O, then unfold the passion of my love.
Surprise her with discourse of my dear faith.
It shall become thee well to act my woes;
She will attend it better in thy youth
Than in a nuncio's of more grave aspect.

VIOLA
I think not so, my lord.

ORSINO Dear lad, believe it.
30 For they shall yet belie thy happy years
That say thou art a man. Diana's lip
Is not more smooth and rubious. Thy small pipe
Is as the maiden's organ, shrill and sound,
And all is semblative a woman's part.
I know thy constellation is right apt
For this affair. Some four or five attend him –
All, if you will; for I myself am best
When least in company. Prosper well in this,
And thou shalt live as freely as thy lord,
40 To call his fortunes thine.

VIOLA I'll do my best
To woo your lady. *(Aside)* Yet, a barful strife!
Whoe'er I woo, myself would be his wife. *Exeunt*

Enter Maria and Feste the Clown

MARIA Nay, either tell me where thou hast been, or I will not open my lips so wide as a bristle may enter, in way of thy excuse. My lady will hang thee for thy absence.

FESTE Let her hang me. He that is well hanged in this world needs to fear no colours.

MARIA Make that good.

FESTE He shall see none to fear.

MARIA A good lenten answer! I can tell thee where that saying was born, of 'I fear no colours'.

FESTE Where, good Mistress Mary? 10

MARIA In the wars; and that may you be bold to say in your foolery.

FESTE Well, God give them wisdom that have it; and those that are fools, let them use their talents.

MARIA Yet you will be hanged for being so long absent; or to be turned away – is not that as good as a hanging to you?

FESTE Many a good hanging prevents a bad marriage; and for turning away, let summer bear it out.

MARIA You are resolute, then? 20

FESTE Not so neither, but I am resolved on two points.

MARIA That if one break, the other will hold; or if both break, your gaskins fall.

FESTE Apt, in good faith, very apt. Well, go thy way, if Sir Toby would leave drinking, thou wert as witty a piece of Eve's flesh as any in Illyria.

MARIA Peace, you rogue, no more o'that. Here comes my lady. Make your excuse wisely, you were best. *Exit*

Enter Olivia with Malvolio and attendants

FESTE Wit, an't be thy will, put me into good fooling. Those wits that think they have thee do very oft prove 30 fools; and I that am sure I lack thee may pass for a wise man. For what says Quinapalus? 'Better a witty fool than a foolish wit'. God bless thee, lady!

OLIVIA Take the fool away.

FESTE Do you not hear, fellows? Take away the lady.

OLIVIA Go to, y'are a dry fool. I'll no more of you. Besides, you grow dishonest.

FESTE Two faults, madonna, that drink and good counsel will amend. For give the dry fool drink, then is the fool not dry. Bid the dishonest man mend himself: if he mend, he is no longer dishonest; if he cannot, let the botcher mend him. Anything that's mended, is but patched: virtue that transgresses is but patched with sin; and sin that amends is but patched with virtue. If that this simple syllogism will serve, so; if it will not, what remedy? As there is no true cuckold but calamity, so beauty's a flower. The lady bade take away the fool; therefore I say again – take her away!

OLIVIA Sir, I bade them take away you.

FESTE Misprision in the highest degree! Lady, *cucullus non facit monachum*; that's as much to say as I wear not motley in my brain. Good madonna, give me leave to prove you a fool.

OLIVIA Can you do it?

FESTE Dexteriously, good madonna.

OLIVIA Make your proof.

FESTE I must catechize you for it, madonna. Good my mouse of virtue, answer me.

OLIVIA Well, sir, for want of other idleness, I'll bide your proof.

FESTE Good madonna, why mourn'st thou?

OLIVIA Good fool, for my brother's death.

FESTE I think his soul is in hell, madonna.

OLIVIA I know his soul is in heaven, fool.

FESTE The more fool, madonna, to mourn for your brother's soul, being in heaven. Take away the fool, gentlemen.

OLIVIA What think you of this fool, Malvolio? Doth he not mend?

MALVOLIO Yes, and shall do, till the pangs of death shake him. Infirmity, that decays the wise, doth ever make the better fool.

FESTE God send you, sir, a speedy infirmity for the better increasing your folly. Sir Toby will be sworn that I am no fox, but he will not pass his word for twopence that you are no fool.

OLIVIA How say you to that, Malvolio?

MALVOLIO I marvel your ladyship takes delight in such a barren rascal. I saw him put down the other day with an ordinary fool that has no more brain than a stone. Look you now, he's out of his guard already; unless you laugh and minister occasion to him, he is gagged. I protest I take these wise men, that crow so at these set kind of fools, no better than the fools' zanies.

OLIVIA O, you are sick of self-love, Malvolio, and taste with a distempered appetite. To be generous, guiltless, and of free disposition, is to take those things for bird-bolts that you deem cannon bullets. There is no slander in an allowed fool, though he do nothing but rail; nor no railing in a known discreet man, though he do nothing but reprove.

FESTE Now Mercury endue thee with leasing, for thou speak'st well of fools.

Enter Maria

MARIA Madam, there is at the gate a young gentleman much desires to speak with you.

OLIVIA From the Count Orsino, is it?

MARIA I know not, madam. 'Tis a fair young man, and well attended.

OLIVIA Who of my people hold him in delay?

MARIA Sir Toby, madam, your kinsman.

OLIVIA Fetch him off, I pray you, he speaks nothing but

madman. Fie on him! Go you, Malvolio. If it be a suit from the Count, I am sick or not at home – what you will, to dismiss it. *Exit Malvolio*

Now you see, sir, how your fooling grows old and people dislike it?

FESTE Thou hast spoke for us, madonna, as if thy eldest son should be a fool; whose skull Jove cram with brains, for – here he comes –

(*Enter Sir Toby*)

110 one of thy kin has a most weak *pia mater*.

OLIVIA By mine honour, half drunk! What is he at the gate, cousin?

SIR TOBY A gentleman.

OLIVIA A gentleman! What gentleman?

SIR TOBY 'Tis a gentleman here – a plague o'these pickle-herring! *(To Feste)* How now, sot!

FESTE Good Sir Toby!

OLIVIA Cousin, cousin, how have you come so early by this lethargy?

120 SIR TOBY Lechery! I defy lechery! There's one at the gate.

OLIVIA Ay, marry, what is he?

SIR TOBY Let him be the devil an he will, I care not. Give me faith, say I. Well, it's all one.

Exit Sir Toby, followed by Maria

OLIVIA What's a drunken man like, fool?

FESTE Like a drowned man, a fool, and a madman. One draught above heat makes him a fool, the second mads him, and a third drowns him.

OLIVIA Go thou and seek the crowner, and let him sit o'

130 my coz, for he's in the third degree of drink – he's drowned. Go, look after him.

FESTE He is but mad yet, madonna, and the fool shall look to the madman. *Exit*

Enter Malvolio

MALVOLIO Madam, yond young fellow swears he will speak with you. I told him you were sick; he takes on him to understand so much, and therefore comes to speak with you. I told him you were asleep; he seems to have a foreknowledge of that too, and therefore comes to speak with you. What is to be said to him, lady? He's fortified against any denial. 140

OLIVIA Tell him, he shall not speak with me.

MALVOLIO He's been told so; and he says he'll stand at your door like a sheriff's post and be the supporter to a bench, but he'll speak with you.

OLIVIA What kind o'man is he?

MALVOLIO Why, of mankind.

OLIVIA What manner of man?

MALVOLIO Of very ill manner; he'll speak with you, will you or no.

OLIVIA Of what personage and years is he? 150

MALVOLIO Not yet old enough for a man, nor young enough for a boy; as a squash is before 'tis a peascod, or a codling when 'tis almost an apple. 'Tis with him in standing water between boy and man. He is very well-favoured, and he speaks very shrewishly. One would think his mother's milk were scarce out of him.

OLIVIA Let him approach. Call in my gentlewoman.

MALVOLIO Gentlewoman, my lady calls. *Exit*

Enter Maria

OLIVIA

Give me my veil. Come, throw it o'er my face.
We'll once more hear Orsino's embassy. 160

Enter Viola

VIOLA The honourable lady of the house, which is she?

OLIVIA Speak to me, I shall answer for her. Your will?

VIOLA Most radiant, exquisite, and unmatchable beauty –

I pray you, tell me if this be the lady of the house, for I never saw her. I would be loath to cast away my speech; for besides that it is excellently well penned, I have taken great pains to con it. Good beauties, let me sustain no scorn. I am very comptible, even to the least sinister usage.

170 OLIVIA Whence came you, sir?

VIOLA I can say little more than I have studied, and that question's out of my part. Good gentle one, give me modest assurance if you be the lady of the house, that I may proceed in my speech.

OLIVIA Are you a comedian?

VIOLA No, my profound heart; and yet, by the very fangs of malice, I swear I am not that I play. Are you the lady of the house?

OLIVIA If I do not usurp myself, I am.

180 VIOLA Most certain, if you are she, you do usurp yourself; for what is yours to bestow is not yours to reserve. But this is from my commission. I will on with my speech in your praise, and then show you the heart of my message.

OLIVIA Come to what is important in't. I forgive you the praise.

VIOLA Alas, I took great pains to study it, and 'tis poetical.

OLIVIA It is the more like to be feigned; I pray you, keep it in. I heard you were saucy at my gates, and allowed your

190 approach rather to wonder at you than to hear you. If you be not mad, be gone; if you have reason, be brief. 'Tis not that time of moon with me, to make one in so skipping a dialogue.

MARIA (*showing Viola the way out*) Will you hoist sail, sir? Here lies your way.

VIOLA No, good swabber, I am to hull here a little longer. Some mollification for your giant, sweet lady! Tell me your mind; I am a messenger.

OLIVIA Sure, you have some hideous matter to deliver, when the courtesy of it is so fearful. Speak your office. 200

VIOLA It alone concerns your ear. I bring no overture of war, no taxation of homage. I hold the olive in my hand; my words are as full of peace as matter.

OLIVIA Yet you began rudely. What are you? What would you?

VIOLA The rudeness that hath appeared in me have I learned from my entertainment. What I am and what I would are as secret as maidenhead; to your ears divinity, to any others profanation.

OLIVIA Give us the place alone. 210

Maria and attendants withdraw

We will hear this divinity. Now, sir, what is your text?

VIOLA Most sweet lady –

OLIVIA A comfortable doctrine, and much may be said of it. Where lies your text?

VIOLA In Orsino's bosom.

OLIVIA In his bosom! In what chapter of his bosom?

VIOLA To answer by the method, in the first of his heart.

OLIVIA O, I have read it; it is heresy. Have you no more to say?

VIOLA Good madam, let me see your face. 220

OLIVIA Have you any commission from your lord to negotiate with my face? You are now out of your text; but we will draw the curtain and show you the picture. Look you, sir, such a one I was this present. Is't not well done?

VIOLA Excellently done – if God did all.

OLIVIA 'Tis in grain, sir, 'twill endure wind and weather.

VIOLA

'Tis beauty truly blent, whose red and white
Nature's own sweet and cunning hand laid on.

230 Lady, you are the cruellest she alive,
If you will lead these graces to the grave,
And leave the world no copy.

OLIVIA O, sir, I will not be so hard-hearted. I will give out divers schedules of my beauty. It shall be inventoried, and every particle and utensil labelled to my will. As, item: two lips, indifferent red; item: two grey eyes, with lids to them; item: one neck, one chin, and so forth. Were you sent hither to praise me?

VIOLA
I see you what you are, you are too proud.
240 But if you were the devil, you are fair.
My lord and master loves you – O, such love
Could be but recompensed, though you were crowned
The nonpareil of beauty!

OLIVIA How does he love me?

VIOLA
With adorations, fertile tears,
With groans that thunder love, with sighs of fire.

OLIVIA
Your lord does know my mind, I cannot love him.
Yet I suppose him virtuous, know him noble,
Of great estate, of fresh and stainless youth,
In voices well divulged, free, learned, and valiant,
250 And in dimension and the shape of nature
A gracious person. But yet I cannot love him.
He might have took his answer long ago.

VIOLA
If I did love you in my master's flame,
With such a suffering, such a deadly life,
In your denial I would find no sense;
I would not understand it.

OLIVIA Why, what would you?

VIOLA

Make me a willow cabin at your gate,
And call upon my soul within the house;
Write loyal cantons of contemnèd love
And sing them loud even in the dead of night; 260
Hallow your name to the reverberate hills
And make the babbling gossip of the air
Cry out 'Olivia!' O, you should not rest
Between the elements of air and earth,
But you should pity me.

OLIVIA You might do much.

What is your parentage?

VIOLA

Above my fortunes, yet my state is well.
I am a gentleman.

OLIVIA Get you to your lord.

I cannot love him. Let him send no more –
Unless, perchance, you come to me again 270
To tell me how he takes it. Fare you well.
I thank you for your pains. Spend this for me.

VIOLA

I am no fee'd post, lady; keep your purse.
My master, not myself, lacks recompense.
Love make his heart of flint, that you shall love,
And let your fervour like my master's be
Placed in contempt. Farewell, fair cruelty! *Exit*

OLIVIA

'What is your parentage?'
'Above my fortunes, yet my state is well.
I am a gentleman.' I'll be sworn thou art. 280
Thy tongue, thy face, thy limbs, actions, and spirit
Do give thee fivefold blazon. Not too fast! soft, soft –
Unless the master were the man. How now?
Even so quickly may one catch the plague?

Methinks I feel this youth's perfections,
With an invisible and subtle stealth,
To creep in at mine eyes. Well, let it be!
What ho, Malvolio!

Enter Malvolio

MALVOLIO

Here, madam, at your service.

OLIVIA

290 Run after that same peevish messenger,
The County's man. He left this ring behind him,
Would I or not. Tell him, I'll none of it.
Desire him not to flatter with his lord,
Nor hold him up with hopes; I am not for him.
If that the youth will come this way tomorrow,
I'll give him reasons for't. Hie thee, Malvolio!

MALVOLIO

Madam, I will. *Exit*

OLIVIA

I do I know not what, and fear to find
Mine eye too great a flatterer for my mind.
300 Fate, show thy force; ourselves we do not owe.
What is decreed must be, and be this so. *Exit*

*

II.1 *Enter Antonio and Sebastian*

ANTONIO Will you stay no longer? Nor will you not that I go with you?

SEBASTIAN By your patience, no. My stars shine darkly over me. The malignancy of my fate might perhaps distemper yours; therefore I shall crave of you your leave, that I may bear my evils alone. It were a bad recompense for your love to lay any of them on you.

ANTONIO Let me yet know of you whither you are bound.

SEBASTIAN No, sooth, sir; my determinate voyage is mere extravagancy. But I perceive in you so excellent a touch 10 of modesty, that you will not extort from me what I am willing to keep in; therefore it charges me in manners the rather to express myself. You must know of me then, Antonio, my name is Sebastian which I called Roderigo. My father was that Sebastian of Messaline whom I know you have heard of. He left behind him myself and a sister, both born in an hour – if the heavens had been pleased, would we had so ended! But you, sir, altered that, for some hour before you took me from the breach of the sea was my sister drowned. 20

ANTONIO Alas the day!

SEBASTIAN A lady, sir, though it was said she much resembled me, was yet of many accounted beautiful. But though I could not with such estimable wonder over-far believe that, yet thus far I will boldly publish her: she bore a mind that envy could not but call fair. She is drowned already, sir, with salt water, though I seem to drown her remembrance again with more.

ANTONIO Pardon me, sir, your bad entertainment.

SEBASTIAN O good Antonio, forgive me your trouble. 30

ANTONIO If you will not murder me for my love, let me be your servant.

SEBASTIAN If you will not undo what you have done – that is, kill him whom you have recovered – desire it not. Fare ye well at once; my bosom is full of kindness, and I am yet so near the manners of my mother that, upon the least occasion more, mine eyes will tell tales of me. I am bound to the Count Orsino's court. Farewell. *Exit*

ANTONIO

The gentleness of all the gods go with thee!
I have many enemies in Orsino's court, 40

Else would I very shortly see thee there –
But come what may, I do adore thee so
That danger shall seem sport, and I will go! *Exit*

II.2 *Enter Viola and Malvolio at several doors*

MALVOLIO Were not you even now with the Countess Olivia?

VIOLA Even now, sir; on a moderate pace I have since arrived but hither.

MALVOLIO She returns this ring to you, sir. You might have saved me my pains, to have taken it away yourself. She adds, moreover, that you should put your lord into a desperate assurance she will none of him; and one thing more, that you be never so hardy to come again in
10 his affairs – unless it be to report your lord's taking of this. Receive it so.

VIOLA She took the ring of me, I'll none of it.

MALVOLIO Come, sir, you peevishly threw it to her, and her will is it should be so returned. If it be worth stooping for, there it lies in your eye; if not, be it his that finds it. *Exit*

VIOLA
I left no ring with her; what means this lady?
Fortune forbid my outside have not charmed her!
She made good view of me, indeed so much
20 That – methought – her eyes had lost her tongue,
For she did speak in starts, distractedly.
She loves me, sure, the cunning of her passion
Invites me in this churlish messenger.
None of my lord's ring? Why, he sent her none.
I am the man! If it be so – as 'tis –
Poor lady, she were better love a dream.
Disguise, I see thou art a wickedness

Wherein the pregnant enemy does much.
How easy is it for the proper false
In women's waxen hearts to set their forms. 30
Alas, our frailty is the cause, not we,
For such as we are made, if such we be.
How will this fadge? My master loves her dearly;
And I, poor monster, fond as much on him;
And she, mistaken, seems to dote on me.
What will become of this? As I am man,
My state is desperate for my master's love.
As I am woman – now, alas the day,
What thriftless sighs shall poor Olivia breathe!
O time, thou must untangle this, not I! 40
It is too hard a knot for me t'untie. *Exit*

Enter Sir Toby and Sir Andrew II.3

SIR TOBY Approach, Sir Andrew. Not to be abed after midnight, is to be up betimes, and *diluculo surgere*, thou knowest –

SIR ANDREW Nay, by my troth, I know not; but I know to be up late is to be up late.

SIR TOBY A false conclusion! I hate it as an unfilled can. To be up after midnight and to go to bed then is early; so that to go to bed after midnight is to go to bed betimes. Does not our lives consist of the four elements?

SIR ANDREW Faith, so they say; but I think it rather consists of eating and drinking. 10

SIR TOBY Thou'rt a scholar. Let us therefore eat and drink. Marian, I say! A stoup of wine!

Enter Feste

SIR ANDREW Here comes the fool, i'faith.

FESTE How now, my hearts! Did you never see the picture of We Three?

SIR TOBY Welcome, ass! Now let's have a catch.

SIR ANDREW By my troth, the fool has an excellent breast. I had rather than forty shillings I had such a leg, and so
20 sweet a breath to sing, as the fool has. In sooth, thou wast in very gracious fooling last night, when thou spok'st of Pigrogromitus, of the Vapians passing the equinoctial of Queubus. 'Twas very good, i'faith. I sent thee sixpence for thy leman, hadst it?

FESTE I did impetticoat thy gratillity; for Malvolio's nose is no whipstock, my lady has a white hand, and the Myrmidons are no bottle-ale houses.

SIR ANDREW Excellent! Why, this is the best fooling, when all is done. Now, a song!

30 SIR TOBY Come on, there is sixpence for you. Let's have a song.

SIR ANDREW There's a testril of me, too. If one knight give a –

FESTE Would you have a love song, or a song of good life?

SIR TOBY A love song! A love song!

SIR ANDREW Ay, ay, I care not for good life.

FESTE (*sings*)

O mistress mine! Where are you roaming?
O, stay and hear: your true love's coming,
That can sing both high and low.
40 Trip no further, pretty sweeting;
Journeys end in lovers meeting,
Every wise man's son doth know.

SIR ANDREW Excellent good, i'faith.

SIR TOBY Good, good.

FESTE (*sings*)

What is love? 'Tis not hereafter;
Present mirth hath present laughter,
What's to come is still unsure.
In delay there lies no plenty –

Then come kiss me, sweet and twenty,
Youth's a stuff will not endure. 50

SIR ANDREW A mellifluous voice, as I am true knight.

SIR TOBY A contagious breath.

SIR ANDREW Very sweet and contagious, i'faith.

SIR TOBY To hear by the nose, it is dulcet in contagion. But shall we make the welkin dance indeed? Shall we rouse the night-owl in a catch that will draw three souls out of one weaver? Shall we do that?

SIR ANDREW An you love me, let's do't. I am dog at a catch.

FESTE By'r lady, sir, and some dogs will catch well. 60

SIR ANDREW Most certain. Let our catch be 'Thou knave'.

FESTE 'Hold thy peace, thou knave', knight? I shall be constrained in't to call thee knave, knight.

SIR ANDREW 'Tis not the first time I have constrained one to call me knave. Begin, fool; it begins (*he sings*) 'Hold thy peace –'

FESTE I shall never begin if I hold my peace.

SIR ANDREW Good, i'faith. Come, begin!

Catch sung. Enter Maria

MARIA What a caterwauling do you keep here! If my lady 70 have not called up her steward Malvolio and bid him turn you out of doors, never trust me.

SIR TOBY My lady's a – Cataian; we are – politicians; Malvolio's a – Peg-a-Ramsey; and (*he sings*)

Three merry men be we!

Am not I consanguineous? Am I not of her blood? Tilly-vally! 'Lady'! (*He sings*)

There dwelt a man in Babylon, lady, lady –

FESTE Beshrew me, the knight's in admirable fooling.

SIR ANDREW Ay, he does well enough if he be disposed, 80 and so do I too. He does it with a better grace, but I do it more natural.

SIR TOBY (*sings*)

O' the twelfth day of December –

MARIA For the love o'God, peace!

Enter Malvolio

MALVOLIO My masters, are you mad? Or what are you? Have you no wit, manners, nor honesty, but to gabble like tinkers at this time of night? Do ye make an alehouse of my lady's house, that ye squeak out your coziers' catches without any mitigation or remorse of voice? Is there no respect of place, persons, nor time in you? 90

SIR TOBY We did keep time, sir, in our catches. Sneck up!

MALVOLIO Sir Toby, I must be round with you. My lady bade me tell you that, though she harbours you as her kinsman, she's nothing allied to your disorders. If you can separate yourself and your misdemeanours, you are welcome to the house. If not, an it would please you to take leave of her, she is very willing to bid you farewell.

SIR TOBY (*sings*)

Farewell, dear heart, since I must needs be gone –

100 MARIA Nay, good Sir Toby!

FESTE (*sings*)

His eyes do show his days are almost done –

MALVOLIO Is't even so!

SIR TOBY (*sings*)

But I will never die –

FESTE (*sings*)

Sir Toby, there you lie –

MALVOLIO This is much credit to you!

SIR TOBY (*sings*)

Shall I bid him go?

FESTE (*sings*)

What an if you do?

SIR TOBY (*sings*)
Shall I bid him go and spare not?
FESTE (*sings*)
O no, no, no, no, you dare not!
SIR TOBY Out o'tune, sir, ye lie. *(To Malvolio)* Art any 110
more than a steward? Dost thou think, because thou art virtuous, there shall be no more cakes and ale?
FESTE Yes, by Saint Anne, and ginger shall be hot i'the mouth, too.
SIR TOBY Th'art i'the right. *(To Malvolio)* Go, sir, rub your chain with crumbs. A stoup of wine, Maria!
MALVOLIO Mistress Mary, if you prized my lady's favour at anything more than contempt, you would not give means for this uncivil rule. She shall know of it, by this hand! *Exit* 120
MARIA Go, shake your ears.
SIR ANDREW 'Twere as good a deed as to drink when a man's a-hungry, to challenge him the field and then to break promise with him and make a fool of him.
SIR TOBY Do't, knight, I'll write thee a challenge; or I'll deliver thy indignation to him by word of mouth.
MARIA Sweet Sir Toby, be patient for tonight. Since the youth of the Count's was today with my lady, she is much out of quiet. For Monsieur Malvolio, let me alone with him. If I do not gull him into a nayword, and make 130
him a common recreation, do not think I have wit enough to lie straight in my bed. I know I can do it.
SIR TOBY Possess us, possess us, tell us something of him.
MARIA Marry, sir, sometimes he is a kind of puritan –
SIR ANDREW O, if I thought that, I'd beat him like a dog.
SIR TOBY What, for being a puritan? Thy exquisite reason, dear knight?
SIR ANDREW I have no exquisite reason for't, but I have reason good enough.

140 MARIA The devil a puritan that he is, or anything, constantly, but a time-pleaser, an affectioned ass that cons state without book and utters it by great swathes; the best persuaded of himself, so crammed, as he thinks, with excellencies, that it is his grounds of faith that all that look on him love him – and on that vice in him will my revenge find notable cause to work.

SIR TOBY What wilt thou do?

MARIA I will drop in his way some obscure epistles of love; wherein, by the colour of his beard, the shape of
150 his leg, the manner of his gait, the expressure of his eye, forehead, and complexion, he shall find himself most feelingly personated. I can write very like my lady, your niece; on a forgotten matter we can hardly make distinction of our hands.

SIR TOBY Excellent! I smell a device.

SIR ANDREW I have't in my nose too.

SIR TOBY He shall think by the letters that thou wilt drop that they come from my niece, and that she's in love with him.

160 MARIA My purpose is indeed a horse of that colour.

SIR ANDREW And your horse now would make him an ass.

MARIA Ass, I doubt not.

SIR ANDREW O, 'twill be admirable!

MARIA Sport royal, I warrant you. I know my physic will work with him. I will plant you two, and let the fool make a third, where he shall find the letter. Observe his construction of it. For this night, to bed, and dream on the event. Farewell. *Exit*

170 SIR TOBY Good night, Penthesilea.

SIR ANDREW Before me, she's a good wench.

SIR TOBY She's a beagle true bred, and one that adores me – what o'that?

SIR ANDREW I was adored once, too.

SIR TOBY Let's to bed, knight. Thou hadst need send for more money.

SIR ANDREW If I cannot recover your niece, I am a foul way out.

SIR TOBY Send for money, knight. If thou hast her not i'the end, call me cut. 180

SIR ANDREW If I do not, never trust me, take it how you will.

SIR TOBY Come, come, I'll go burn some sack, 'tis too late to go to bed now. Come, knight; come, knight.

Exeunt

Enter Orsino, Viola, Curio, and others II.4

ORSINO

Give me some music! Now, good morrow, friends!
Now, good Cesario, but that piece of song,
That old and antique song we heard last night.
Methought it did relieve my passion much,
More than light airs and recollected terms
Of these most brisk and giddy-pacèd times.
Come, but one verse.

CURIO He is not here, so please your lordship, that should sing it.

ORSINO Who was it? 10

CURIO Feste the jester, my lord, a fool that the Lady Olivia's father took much delight in. He is about the house.

ORSINO Seek him out, and play the tune the while.

Exit Curio

Music plays

Come hither, boy. If ever thou shalt love,
In the sweet pangs of it, remember me.

For such as I am, all true lovers are:
Unstaid and skittish in all motions else,
Save in the constant image of the creature
20 That is beloved. How dost thou like this tune?

VIOLA
It gives a very echo to the seat
Where love is throned.

ORSINO Thou dost speak masterly.
My life upon't, young though thou art, thine eye
Hath stayed upon some favour that it loves.
Hath it not, boy?

VIOLA A little, by your favour.

ORSINO
What kind of woman is't?

VIOLA Of your complexion.

ORSINO
She is not worth thee, then. What years, i'faith?

VIOLA
About your years, my lord.

ORSINO
Too old, by heaven. Let still the woman take
30 An elder than herself; so wears she to him;
So sways she level in her husband's heart.
For, boy, however we do praise ourselves,
Our fancies are more giddy and unfirm,
More longing, wavering, sooner lost and worn,
Than women's are.

VIOLA I think it well, my lord.

ORSINO
Then let thy love be younger than thyself,
Or thy affection cannot hold the bent.
For women are as roses whose fair flower,
Being once displayed, doth fall that very hour.

VIOLA
40 And so they are. Alas, that they are so,

To die, even when they to perfection grow.

Enter Curio and Feste

ORSINO

O, fellow, come, the song we had last night.
Mark it, Cesario; it is old and plain.
The spinsters, and the knitters in the sun,
And the free maids that weave their thread with bones,
Do use to chant it. It is silly sooth,
And dallies with the innocence of love
Like the old age.

FESTE

Are you ready, sir?

ORSINO Ay, prithee sing.

Music plays

FESTE (*sings*)

Come away, come away, death, 50
And in sad cypress let me be laid.
Fie away, fie away, breath!
I am slain by a fair cruel maid.
My shroud of white, stuck all with yew,
O, prepare it!
My part of death, no one so true
Did share it.

Not a flower, not a flower sweet
On my black coffin let there be strewn.
Not a friend, not a friend greet 60
My poor corpse, where my bones shall be thrown.
A thousand thousand sighs to save,
Lay me, O, where
Sad true lover never find my grave
To weep there.

ORSINO There's for thy pains.

He gives Feste money

FESTE No pains, sir. I take pleasure in singing, sir.

ORSINO I'll pay thy pleasure, then.

FESTE Truly, sir, and pleasure will be paid, one time or
70 another.

ORSINO Give me now leave, to leave thee.

FESTE Now the melancholy god protect thee, and the tailor make thy doublet of changeable taffeta, for thy mind is a very opal. I would have men of such constancy put to sea, that their business might be everything, and their intent everywhere; for that's it that always makes a good voyage of nothing. Farewell.

Exit Feste

ORSINO

Let all the rest give place.

Curio and attendants withdraw

Once more, Cesario,

Get thee to yond same sovereign cruelty.

80 Tell her my love, more noble than the world,

Prizes not quantity of dirty lands.

The parts that fortune hath bestowed upon her

Tell her I hold as giddily as fortune.

But 'tis that miracle and queen of gems

That nature pranks her in, attracts my soul.

VIOLA

But if she cannot love you, sir?

ORSINO

It cannot be so answered.

VIOLA Sooth, but you must.

Say that some lady, as perhaps there is,

Hath for your love as great a pang of heart

90 As you have for Olivia. You cannot love her.

You tell her so. Must she not then be answered?

ORSINO

There is no woman's sides

Can bide the beating of so strong a passion

As love doth give my heart; no woman's heart
So big to hold so much, they lack retention.
Alas, their love may be called appetite,
No motion of the liver, but the palate,
That suffer surfeit, cloyment, and revolt.
But mine is all as hungry as the sea,
And can digest as much. Make no compare 100
Between that love a woman can bear me
And that I owe Olivia.

VIOLA
Ay, but I know –

ORSINO
What dost thou know?

VIOLA
Too well what love women to men may owe.
In faith, they are as true of heart as we.
My father had a daughter loved a man –
As it might be perhaps, were I a woman,
I should your lordship.

ORSINO
And what's her history?

VIOLA
A blank, my lord. She never told her love,
But let concealment, like a worm i'the bud, 110
Feed on her damask cheek. She pined in thought,
And with a green and yellow melancholy,
She sat like Patience on a monument,
Smiling at grief. Was not this love indeed?
We men may say more, swear more, but indeed
Our shows are more than will; for still we prove
Much in our vows, but little in our love.

ORSINO
But died thy sister of her love, my boy?

VIOLA
I am all the daughters of my father's house,
And all the brothers too; and yet, I know not. . . . 120

Sir, shall I to this lady?

ORSINO Ay, that's the theme.

To her in haste; give her this jewel; say
My love can give no place, bide no denay. *Exeunt*

II.5 *Enter Sir Toby, Sir Andrew, and Fabian*

SIR TOBY Come thy ways, Signor Fabian.

FABIAN Nay, I'll come. If I lose a scruple of this sport, let me be boiled to death with melancholy.

SIR TOBY Wouldst thou not be glad to have the niggardly, rascally sheep-biter come by some notable shame?

FABIAN I would exult, man. You know he brought me out o'favour with my lady about a bear-baiting here.

SIR TOBY To anger him, we'll have the bear again, and
10 we will fool him black and blue – shall we not, Sir Andrew?

SIR ANDREW An we do not, it is pity of our lives.

Enter Maria

SIR TOBY Here comes the little villain. How now, my metal of India?

MARIA Get ye all three into the box-tree. Malvolio's coming down this walk, he has been yonder i'the sun practising behaviour to his own shadow this half-hour. Observe him, for the love of mockery, for I know this letter will make a contemplative idiot of him. Close, in
20 the name of jesting!

The men hide. Maria throws down a letter

Lie thou there – for here comes the trout that must be caught with tickling. *Exit*

Enter Malvolio

MALVOLIO 'Tis but fortune, all is fortune. Maria once told me she did affect me; and I have heard herself come thus near, that should she fancy, it should be one of my complexion. Besides, she uses me with a more exalted respect than anyone else that follows her. What should I think on't?

SIR TOBY Here's an overweening rogue!

FABIAN O, peace! Contemplation makes a rare turkey-cock of him; how he jets under his advanced plumes! 30

SIR ANDREW 'Slight, I could so beat the rogue!

SIR TOBY Peace, I say!

MALVOLIO To be Count Malvolio . . .

SIR TOBY Ah, rogue!

SIR ANDREW Pistol him, pistol him!

SIR TOBY Peace, peace!

MALVOLIO There is example for't. The lady of the Strachy married the yeoman of the wardrobe.

SIR ANDREW Fie on him! Jezebel! 40

FABIAN O, peace! Now he's deeply in. Look how imagination blows him.

MALVOLIO Having been three months married to her, sitting in my state . . .

SIR TOBY O for a stone-bow to hit him in the eye!

MALVOLIO Calling my officers about me, in my branched velvet gown, having come from a day-bed, where I have left Olivia sleeping . . .

SIR TOBY Fire and brimstone!

FABIAN O, peace, peace! 50

MALVOLIO And then to have the humour of state; and after a demure travel of regard – telling them I know my place, as I would they should do theirs – to ask for my kinsman Toby.

SIR TOBY Bolts and shackles!

FABIAN O, peace, peace, peace! Now, now!

MALVOLIO Seven of my people, with an obedient start, make out for him. I frown the while, and perchance

wind up my watch, or play with my (*fingering his*
60 *steward's chain of office*) – some rich jewel. Toby
approaches, curtsies there to me . . .

SIR TOBY Shall this fellow live?

FABIAN Though our silence be drawn from us with cars,
yet peace!

MALVOLIO I extend my hand to him thus – quenching
my familiar smile with an austere regard of control . . .

SIR TOBY And does not Toby take you a blow o'the lips
then?

MALVOLIO Saying, Cousin Toby, my fortunes having
70 cast me on your niece give me this prerogative of
speech . . .

SIR TOBY What, what!

MALVOLIO You must amend your drunkenness.

SIR TOBY Out, scab!

FABIAN Nay, patience, or we break the sinews of our plot.

MALVOLIO Besides, you waste the treasure of your time
with a foolish knight . . .

SIR ANDREW That's me, I warrant you.

MALVOLIO One Sir Andrew.

80 SIR ANDREW I knew 'twas I, for many do call me fool.

MALVOLIO (*picks up the letter*) What employment have
we here?

FABIAN Now is the woodcock near the gin.

SIR TOBY O, peace, and the spirit of humours intimate
reading aloud to him!

MALVOLIO By my life, this is my lady's hand. These be
her very C's, her U's and her T's; and thus makes she
her great P's. It is, in contempt of question, her hand.

SIR ANDREW Her C's, her U's and her T's? Why that?

MALVOLIO (*reads*)

90 *To the unknown beloved this, and my good wishes.*

Her very phrases! By your leave, wax. Soft! and the

impressure her Lucrece, with which she uses to seal.
'Tis my lady! To whom should this be?

FABIAN This wins him, liver and all.

MALVOLIO (*reads*)

Jove knows I love;
But who?
Lips, do not move;
No man must know.

'No man must know'! What follows? The numbers altered! 'No man must know'! If this should be thee, 100
Malvolio!

SIR TOBY Marry, hang thee, brock!

MALVOLIO (*reads*)

I may command where I adore;
But silence, like a Lucrece' knife,
With bloodless stroke my heart doth gore;
M.O.A.I. doth sway my life.

FABIAN A fustian riddle!

SIR TOBY Excellent wench, say I!

MALVOLIO 'M.O.A.I. doth sway my life.' Nay, but first let me see, let me see, let me see. . . . 110

FABIAN What dish o'poison has she dressed him!

SIR TOBY And with what wing the staniel checks at it!

MALVOLIO 'I may command where I adore'. Why, she may command me. I serve her, she is my lady. Why, this is evident to any formal capacity. There is no obstruction in this. And the end: what should that alphabetical position portend? If I could make that resemble something in me. . . . Softly, 'M.O.A.I.' . . .

SIR TOBY O, ay, make up that. He is now at a cold scent.

FABIAN Sowter will cry upon't for all this, though it be as 120
rank as a fox.

MALVOLIO M . . . Malvolio! M! Why, that begins my name!

FABIAN Did not I say he would work it out? The cur is excellent at faults.

MALVOLIO M! But then there is no consonancy in the sequel that suffers under probation. A should follow, but O does.

FABIAN And O shall end, I hope.

130 SIR TOBY Ay, or I'll cudgel him and make him cry O.

MALVOLIO And then I comes behind.

FABIAN Ay, an you had any eye behind you, you might see more detraction at your heels than fortunes before you.

MALVOLIO M.O.A.I. This simulation is not as the former. And yet, to crush this a little, it would bow to me, for every one of these letters are in my name. Soft! Here follows prose.

He reads

If this fall into thy hand, revolve. In my stars I am above
140 *thee, but be not afraid of greatness. Some are born great, some achieve greatness, and some have greatness thrust upon 'em. Thy fates open their hands, let thy blood and spirit embrace them; and to inure thyself to what thou art like to be, cast thy humble slough and appear fresh. Be opposite with a kinsman, surly with servants. Let thy tongue tang arguments of state. Put thyself into the trick of singularity. She thus advises thee that sighs for thee. Remember who commended thy yellow stockings and wished to see thee ever cross-gartered. I say, remember. Go to, thou*
150 *art made if thou desirest to be so. If not, let me see thee a steward still, the fellow of servants, and not worthy to touch Fortune's fingers. Farewell. She that would alter services with thee, The Fortunate Unhappy.*

Daylight and champain discovers not more! This is open. I will be proud, I will read politic authors, I will baffle Sir Toby, I will wash off gross acquaintance, I will be point-devise the very man. I do not now fool myself, to let imagination jade me; for every reason excites to this, that my lady loves me. She did commend my yellow stockings of late, she did praise my leg being cross-gartered; and in this she manifests herself to my love and with a kind of injunction drives me to these habits of her liking. I thank my stars, I am happy! I will be strange, stout, in yellow stockings and cross-gartered, even with the swiftness of putting on. Jove and my stars be praised! Here is yet a postcript. 160

He reads

Thou canst not choose but know who I am. If thou entertainest my love, let it appear in thy smiling, thy smiles become thee well. Therefore in my presence still smile, dear my sweet, I prithee. 170

Jove, I thank thee! I will smile. I will do everything that thou wilt have me! *Exit*

FABIAN I will not give my part of this sport for a pension of thousands to be paid from the Sophy.

SIR TOBY I could marry this wench for this device.

SIR ANDREW So could I too.

SIR TOBY And ask no other dowry with her but such another jest.

SIR ANDREW Nor I neither.

Enter Maria

FABIAN Here comes my noble gull-catcher. 180

SIR TOBY Wilt thou set thy foot o' my neck?

SIR ANDREW Or o' mine either?

SIR TOBY Shall I play my freedom at tray-trip and become thy bondslave?

SIR ANDREW I'faith, or I either?

SIR TOBY Why, thou hast put him in such a dream, that

when the image of it leaves him, he must run mad.

MARIA Nay, but say true: does it work upon him?

SIR TOBY Like aqua-vitae with a midwife.

190 MARIA If you will then see the fruits of the sport, mark his first approach before my lady. He will come to her in yellow stockings, and 'tis a colour she abhors; and cross-gartered, a fashion she detests; and he will smile upon her, which will now be so unsuitable to her disposition – being addicted to a melancholy as she is – that it cannot but turn him into a notable contempt. If you will see it, follow me.

SIR TOBY To the gates of Tartar, thou most excellent devil of wit!

200 SIR ANDREW I'll make one too. *Exeunt*

*

III.1 *Enter at different entrances Viola, and Feste playing his pipe and tabor*

VIOLA Save thee, friend, and thy music. Dost thou live by thy tabor?

FESTE No, sir, I live by the church.

VIOLA Art thou a Churchman?

FESTE No such matter, sir; I do live by the church. For I do live at my house, and my house doth stand by the church.

VIOLA So thou mayst say the king lies by a beggar, if a beggar dwell near him; or the Church stands by thy

10 tabor, if thy tabor stand by the church.

FESTE You have said, sir. To see this age! A sentence is but a cheveril glove to a good wit; how quickly the wrong side may be turned outward!

VIOLA Nay, that's certain. They that dally nicely with

words may quickly make them wanton.

FESTE I would therefore my sister had had no name, sir.

VIOLA Why, man?

FESTE Why, sir, her name's a word, and to dally with that word might make my sister wanton. But indeed, words are very rascals, since bonds disgraced them. 20

VIOLA Thy reason, man?

FESTE Troth, sir, I can yield you none without words, and words are grown so false, I am loath to prove reason with them.

VIOLA I warrant thou art a merry fellow, and car'st for nothing.

FESTE Not so, sir. I do care for something; but in my conscience, sir, I do not care for you. If that be to care for nothing, sir, I would it would make you invisible.

VIOLA Art not thou the Lady Olivia's fool? 30

FESTE No indeed, sir, the Lady Olivia has no folly. She will keep no fool, sir, till she be married, and fools are as like husbands as pilchers are to herrings; the husband's the bigger. I am indeed not her fool, but her corrupter of words.

VIOLA I saw thee late at the Count Orsino's.

FESTE Foolery, sir, does walk about the orb like the sun, it shines everywhere. I would be sorry, sir, but the fool should be as oft with your master as with my mistress. I think I saw your wisdom there? 40

VIOLA Nay, an thou pass upon me, I'll no more with thee. Hold, there's expenses for thee!

She gives him a coin

FESTE Now Jove, in his next commodity of hair, send thee a beard!

VIOLA By my troth, I'll tell thee, I am almost sick for one – (*aside*) though I would not have it grow on my chin. Is thy lady within?

FESTE Would not a pair of these have bred, sir?

VIOLA Yes, being kept together and put to use.

50 FESTE I would play Lord Pandarus of Phrygia, sir, to bring a Cressida to this Troilus.

VIOLA I understand you, sir; 'tis well begged.

She gives another coin

FESTE The matter, I hope, is not great, sir, begging but a beggar – Cressida was a beggar. My lady is within, sir. I will conster to them whence you come. Who you are and what you would are out of my welkin – I might say 'element', but the word is overworn. *Exit*

VIOLA

This fellow is wise enough to play the fool;
And to do that well craves a kind of wit.
60 He must observe their mood on whom he jests,
The quality of persons, and the time,
And, like the haggard, check at every feather
That comes before his eye. This is a practice
As full of labour as a wise man's art.
For folly that he wisely shows is fit;
But wise men, folly-fallen, quite taint their wit.

Enter Sir Toby and Sir Andrew

SIR TOBY Save you, gentleman!

VIOLA And you, sir!

SIR ANDREW *Dieu vous garde, monsieur!*

70 VIOLA *Et vous aussi; votre serviteur!*

SIR ANDREW I hope, sir, you are, and I am yours.

SIR TOBY Will you encounter the house? My niece is desirous you should enter, if your trade be to her.

VIOLA I am bound to your niece, sir. I mean, she is the list of my voyage.

SIR TOBY Taste your legs, sir; put them to motion.

VIOLA My legs do better under-stand me, sir, than I understand what you mean by bidding me taste my legs.

SIR TOBY I mean to go, sir, to enter.

VIOLA I will answer you with gate and entrance. 80

Enter Olivia and Maria

But we are prevented. *(To Olivia)* Most excellent, accomplished lady, the heavens rain odours on you!

SIR ANDREW (*aside*) That youth's a rare courtier. 'Rain odours'! Well!

VIOLA My matter hath no voice, lady, but to your own most pregnant and vouchsafed ear.

SIR ANDREW 'Odours'; 'pregnant'; and 'vouchsafed'. I'll get 'em all three all ready.

OLIVIA Let the garden door be shut and leave me to my hearing. 90

Exeunt Sir Toby and Maria, Sir Andrew lingering before he, too, leaves

Give me your hand, sir.

VIOLA

My duty, madam, and most humble service!

OLIVIA

What is your name?

VIOLA

Cesario is your servant's name, fair princess.

OLIVIA

My servant, sir? 'Twas never merry world
Since lowly feigning was called compliment.
Y'are servant to the Count Orsino, youth.

VIOLA

And he is yours, and his must needs be yours.
Your servant's servant is your servant, madam.

OLIVIA

For him, I think not on him. For his thoughts, 100
Would they were blanks rather than filled with me.

VIOLA

Madam, I come to whet your gentle thoughts

On his behalf –

OLIVIA O, by your leave, I pray you.

I bade you never speak again of him.
But would you undertake another suit,
I had rather hear you to solicit that
Than music from the spheres.

VIOLA Dear lady –

OLIVIA

Give me leave, beseech you. I did send,
After the last enchantment you did here,
110 A ring in chase of you. So did I abuse
Myself, my servant, and, I fear me, you.
Under your hard construction must I sit,
To force that on you in a shameful cunning
Which you knew none of yours. What might you think?
Have you not set mine honour at the stake,
And baited it with all th'unmuzzled thoughts
That tyrannous heart can think? To one of your receiving
Enough is shown; a cypress, not a bosom,
Hides my heart. So let me hear you speak.

VIOLA

120 I pity you.

OLIVIA That's a degree to love.

VIOLA

No, not a grize; for 'tis a vulgar proof
That very oft we pity enemies.

OLIVIA

Why, then, methinks 'tis time to smile again.
O world, how apt the poor are to be proud!
If one should be a prey, how much the better
To fall before the lion than the wolf!

Clock strikes

The clock upbraids me with the waste of time.

Be not afraid, good youth; I will not have you.
And yet, when wit and youth is come to harvest,
Your wife is like to reap a proper man. 130
There lies your way, due west.

VIOLA
Then westward ho!
Grace and good disposition attend your ladyship.
You'll nothing, madam, to my lord by me?

OLIVIA
Stay.
I prithee, tell me what thou think'st of me?

VIOLA
That you do think you are not what you are.

OLIVIA
If I think so, I think the same of you.

VIOLA
Then think you right; I am not what I am.

OLIVIA
I would you were as I would have you be.

VIOLA
Would it be better, madam, than I am? 140
I wish it might, for now I am your fool.

OLIVIA (*aside*)
O, what a deal of scorn looks beautiful
In the contempt and anger of his lip!
A murderous guilt shows not itself more soon
Than love that would seem hid; love's night is noon.
(To Viola) Cesario, by the roses of the spring,
By maidhood, honour, truth, and everything,
I love thee so that, maugre all thy pride,
Nor wit nor reason can my passion hide.
Do not extort thy reasons from this clause: 150
For that I woo, thou therefore hast no cause.
But rather reason thus with reason fetter:
Love sought, is good; but given unsought, is better.

VIOLA

By innocence I swear, and by my youth,
I have one heart, one bosom, and one truth.
And that no woman has, nor never none
Shall mistress be of it, save I alone.
And so, adieu, good madam; never more
Will I my master's tears to you deplore.

OLIVIA

160 Yet come again; for thou perhaps mayst move
That heart, which now abhors, to like his love.

Exeunt

III.2 *Enter Sir Toby, Sir Andrew, and Fabian*

SIR ANDREW No, faith, I'll not stay a jot longer.

SIR TOBY Thy reason, dear venom, give thy reason.

FABIAN You must needs yield your reason, Sir Andrew.

SIR ANDREW Marry, I saw your niece do more favours to the Count's servingman than ever she bestowed upon me. I saw't i'the orchard.

SIR TOBY Did she see thee the while, old boy, tell me that?

SIR ANDREW As plain as I see you now.

10 FABIAN This was a great argument of love in her toward you.

SIR ANDREW 'Slight! Will you make an ass o'me?

FABIAN I will prove it legitimate, sir, upon the oaths of judgement and reason.

SIR TOBY And they have been grand-jury men since before Noah was a sailor.

FABIAN She did show favour to the youth in your sight only to exasperate you, to awake your dormouse valour, to put fire in your heart and brimstone in your liver. You
20 should then have accosted her, and with some excellent

jests fire-new from the mint, you should have banged the youth into dumbness. This was looked for at your hand, and this was baulked. The double gilt of this opportunity you let time wash off, and you are now sailed into the north of my lady's opinion; where you will hang like an icicle on a Dutchman's beard, unless you do redeem it by some laudable attempt either of valour or policy.

SIR ANDREW An't be any way, it must be with valour, for policy I hate. I had as lief be a Brownist as a politician. 30

SIR TOBY Why then, build me thy fortunes upon the basis of valour. Challenge me the Count's youth to fight with him; hurt him in eleven places; my niece shall take note of it – and, assure thyself, there is no love-broker in the world can more prevail in man's commendation with woman than report of valour.

FABIAN There is no way but this, Sir Andrew.

SIR ANDREW Will either of you bear me a challenge to him?

SIR TOBY Go, write it in a martial hand. Be curst and brief. It is no matter how witty, so it be eloquent and full of invention. Taunt him with the licence of ink. If thou 'thou'-est him some thrice it shall not be amiss, and as many lies as will lie in thy sheet of paper – although the sheet were big enough for the bed of Ware in England, set 'em down, go about it. Let there be gall enough in thy ink, though thou write with a goose pen, no matter. About it! 40

SIR ANDREW Where shall I find you?

SIR TOBY We'll call thee at thy cubiculo. Go! 50

Exit Sir Andrew

FABIAN This is a dear manikin to you, Sir Toby.

SIR TOBY I have been dear to him, lad, some two thousand strong or so.

FABIAN We shall have a rare letter from him. But you'll not deliver it?

SIR TOBY Never trust me then – and by all means stir on the youth to an answer. I think oxen and wain-ropes cannot hale them together. For Andrew, if he were opened and you find so much blood in his liver as will
60 clog the foot of a flea, I'll eat the rest of the anatomy.

FABIAN And his opposite the youth bears in his visage no great presage of cruelty.

Enter Maria

SIR TOBY Look where the youngest wren of nine comes.

MARIA If you desire the spleen, and will laugh yourselves into stitches, follow me. Yond gull Malvolio is turned heathen, a very renegado; for there is no Christian, that means to be saved by believing rightly, can ever believe such impossible passages of grossness. He's in yellow stockings!

70 SIR TOBY And cross-gartered?

MARIA Most villainously; like a pedant that keeps a school i'the church. I have dogged him like his murderer. He does obey every point of the letter that I dropped to betray him. He does smile his face into more lines than is in the new map with the augmentation of the Indies. You have not seen such a thing as 'tis. I can hardly forbear hurling things at him; I know my lady will strike him. If she do, he'll smile, and take it for a great favour.

80 SIR TOBY Come, bring us, bring us where he is. *Exeunt*

III.3 *Enter Sebastian and Antonio*

SEBASTIAN

I would not by my will have troubled you.
But since you make your pleasure of your pains,

I will no further chide you.

ANTONIO

I could not stay behind you. My desire,
More sharp than filèd steel, did spur me forth,
And not all love to see you – though so much
As might have drawn one to a longer voyage –
But jealousy what might befall your travel,
Being skill-less in these parts; which to a stranger,
Unguided and unfriended, often prove
Rough and unhospitable. My willing love, 10
The rather by these arguments of fear,
Set forth in your pursuit.

SEBASTIAN My kind Antonio,
I can no other answer make but thanks,
And thanks. And ever oft good turns
Are shuffled off with such uncurrent pay.
But were my worth, as is my conscience, firm,
You should find better dealing. What's to do?
Shall we go see the reliques of this town?

ANTONIO

Tomorrow, sir; best first go see your lodging. 20

SEBASTIAN

I am not weary, and 'tis long to night.
I pray you, let us satisfy our eyes
With the memorials and the things of fame
That do renown this city.

ANTONIO

Would you'd pardon me.
I do not without danger walk these streets.
Once in a seafight 'gainst the Count his galleys
I did some service – of such note indeed
That, were I ta'en here, it would scarce be answered.

SEBASTIAN

Belike you slew great number of his people? 30

ANTONIO
Th'offence is not of such a bloody nature,
Albeit the quality of the time and quarrel
Might well have given us bloody argument.
It might have since been answered in repaying
What we took from them, which, for traffic's sake,
Most of our city did. Only myself stood out.
For which, if I be lapsèd in this place,
I shall pay dear.

SEBASTIAN Do not then walk too open.

ANTONIO
It doth not fit me. Hold, sir, here's my purse.
40 In the south suburbs, at the Elephant,
Is best to lodge. I will bespeak our diet
Whiles you beguile the time, and feed your knowledge
With viewing of the town. There shall you have me.

SEBASTIAN
Why I your purse?

ANTONIO
Haply your eye shall light upon some toy
You have desire to purchase; and your store,
I think, is not for idle markets, sir.

SEBASTIAN
I'll be your purse-bearer, and leave you for
An hour.

ANTONIO To th'Elephant.

SEBASTIAN I do remember.

Exeunt separately

III.4 *Enter Olivia and Maria*

OLIVIA (*aside*)
I have sent after him, he says he'll come.
How shall I feast him? What bestow of him?

For youth is bought more oft than begged or borrowed.
I speak too loud.
(To Maria) Where's Malvolio? He is sad and civil,
And suits well for a servant with my fortunes.
Where is Malvolio?

MARIA He's coming, madam, but in very strange manner.
He is sure possessed, madam.

OLIVIA Why, what's the matter? Does he rave? 10

MARIA No, madam, he does nothing but smile. Your ladyship were best to have some guard about you, if he come, for sure the man is tainted in's wits.

OLIVIA
Go, call him hither. *Exit Maria*
I am as mad as he
If sad and merry madness equal be.

Enter Malvolio and Maria

How now, Malvolio?

MALVOLIO Sweet lady! Ho! Ho!

OLIVIA Smil'st thou? I sent for thee upon a sad occasion.

MALVOLIO Sad, lady? I could be sad; this does make some obstruction in the blood, this cross-gartering – but 20 what of that? If it please the eye of one, it is with me as the very true sonnet is: 'Please one and please all'.

OLIVIA Why, how dost thou, man? What is the matter with thee?

MALVOLIO Not black in my mind, though yellow in my legs. It did come to his hands; and commands shall be executed. I think we do know the sweet Roman hand.

OLIVIA Wilt thou go to bed, Malvolio?

MALVOLIO To bed! 'Ay, sweetheart, and I'll come to thee!' 30

OLIVIA God comfort thee! Why dost thou smile so, and kiss thy hand so oft?

MARIA How do you, Malvolio?

MALVOLIO At your request? Yes; nightingales answer daws.

MARIA Why appear you with this ridiculous boldness before my lady?

MALVOLIO 'Be not afraid of greatness.' 'Twas well writ.

OLIVIA What mean'st thou by that, Malvolio?

40 MALVOLIO 'Some are born great –'

OLIVIA Ha?

MALVOLIO 'Some achieve greatness –'

OLIVIA What sayst thou?

MALVOLIO 'And some have greatness thrust upon them.'

OLIVIA Heaven restore thee!

MALVOLIO 'Remember who commended thy yellow stockings –'

OLIVIA Thy yellow stockings?

50 MALVOLIO '– and wished to see thee cross-gartered.'

OLIVIA Cross-gartered?

MALVOLIO 'Go to, thou art made if thou desir'st to be so.'

OLIVIA Am I maid!

MALVOLIO 'If not, let me see thee a servant still.'

OLIVIA Why, this is very midsummer madness.

Enter a Servant

SERVANT Madam, the young gentleman of the Count Orsino's is returned. I could hardly entreat him back. He attends your ladyship's pleasure.

60 OLIVIA I'll come to him. *Exit Servant*

Good Maria, let this fellow be looked to. Where's my cousin Toby? Let some of my people have a special care of him. I would not have him miscarry for the half of my dowry. *Exeunt Olivia and Maria different ways*

MALVOLIO O ho! Do you come near me now? No worse man than Sir Toby to look to me! This concurs directly with the letter. She sends him on purpose, that I may appear stubborn to him; for she incites me to that in the letter. 'Cast thy humble slough,' says she. 'Be opposite with a kinsman, surly with servants, let thy tongue tang with arguments of state, put thyself into the trick of singularity' – and consequently sets down the manner how: as, a sad face, a reverend carriage, a slow tongue, in the habit of some sir of note, and so forth. I have limed her! But it is Jove's doing, and Jove make me thankful! And when she went away now – 'let this fellow be looked to'. Fellow! Not 'Malvolio', nor after my degree, but 'fellow'! Why, everything adheres together, that no dram of a scruple, no scruple of a scruple, no obstacle, no incredulous or unsafe circumstance – what can be said? – nothing that can be, can come between me and the full prospect of my hopes. Well, Jove, not I, is the doer of this, and he is to be thanked. 70 80

Enter Sir Toby, Fabian, and Maria

SIR TOBY Which way is he, in the name of sanctity? If all the devils of hell be drawn in little and Legion himself possessed him, yet I'll speak to him.

FABIAN Here he is, here he is. How is't with you, sir? How is't with you, man?

MALVOLIO Go off, I discard you. Let me enjoy my private. Go off. 90

MARIA Lo, how hollow the fiend speaks within him. Did not I tell you? Sir Toby, my lady prays you to have a care of him.

MALVOLIO Ah ha! Does she so!

SIR TOBY Go to, go to! Peace, peace, we must deal gently with him. Let me alone. How do you, Malvolio? How is't with you? What, man, defy the devil! Consider, he's an enemy to mankind.

MALVOLIO Do you know what you say?

100 MARIA La you, an you speak ill of the devil, how he takes it at heart! Pray God he be not bewitched!

FABIAN Carry his water to the wisewoman.

MARIA Marry, and it shall be done tomorrow morning, if I live. My lady would not lose him, for more than I'll say.

MALVOLIO How now, mistress?

MARIA O Lord!

SIR TOBY Prithee, hold thy peace, this is not the way. Do you not see you move him? Let me alone with him.

110 FABIAN No way but gentleness, gently, gently. The fiend is rough, and will not be roughly used.

SIR TOBY Why, how now, my bawcock? How dost thou, chuck?

MALVOLIO Sir!

SIR TOBY Ay, biddy, come with me. What, man, 'tis not for gravity to play at cherry-pit with Satan. Hang him, foul collier!

MARIA Get him to say his prayers, good Sir Toby; get him to pray.

120 MALVOLIO My prayers, minx!

MARIA No, I warrant you, he will not hear of godliness.

MALVOLIO Go, hang yourselves all. You are idle, shallow things; I am not of your element. You shall know more hereafter. *Exit Malvolio*

SIR TOBY Is't possible?

FABIAN If this were played upon a stage now, I could condemn it as an improbable fiction.

SIR TOBY His very genius hath taken the infection of the device, man.

130 MARIA Nay, pursue him now, lest the device take air, and taint.

FABIAN Why, we shall make him mad indeed.

MARIA The house will be the quieter.

SIR TOBY Come, we'll have him in a dark room and bound. My niece is already in the belief that he's mad. We may carry it thus for our pleasure and his penance till our very pastime, tired out of breath, prompt us to have mercy on him; at which time, we will bring the device to the bar, and crown thee for a finder of madmen. But see, but see! 140

Enter Sir Andrew

FABIAN More matter for a May morning!

SIR ANDREW Here's the challenge, read it. I warrant there's vinegar and pepper in't.

FABIAN Is't so saucy?

SIR ANDREW Ay, is't, I warrant him. Do but read.

SIR TOBY Give me.

He reads

Youth, whatsoever thou art, thou art but a scurvy fellow.

FABIAN Good and valiant.

SIR TOBY (*reads*) *Wonder not, nor admire not in thy mind, why I do call thee so, for I will show thee no reason for't.* 150

FABIAN A good note, that keeps you from the blow of the law.

SIR TOBY (*reads*) *Thou com'st to the Lady Olivia, and in my sight she uses thee kindly. But thou liest in thy throat; that is not the matter I challenge thee for.*

FABIAN Very brief, and to exceeding good sense – (*aside*) less!

SIR TOBY (*reads*) *I will waylay thee going home; where, if it be thy chance to kill me –*

FABIAN Good! 160

SIR TOBY (*reads*) *thou kill'st me like a rogue and a villain.*

FABIAN Still you keep o' the windy side of the law; good.

SIR TOBY (*reads*) *Fare thee well, and God have mercy upon one of our souls. He may have mercy upon mine, but my hope is better – and so, look to thyself. Thy friend as thou usest him, and thy sworn enemy, Andrew Aguecheek.* If this letter move him not, his legs cannot. I'll give't him.

170 MARIA You may have very fit occasion for't. He is now in some commerce with my lady, and will by and by depart.

SIR TOBY Go, Sir Andrew. Scout me for him at the corner of the orchard like a bum-baily. So soon as ever thou seest him, draw, and as thou drawest, swear horrible; for it comes to pass oft that a terrible oath, with a swaggering accent sharply twanged off, gives manhood more approbation than ever proof itself would have earned him. Away!

180 SIR ANDREW Nay, let me alone for swearing. *Exit*

SIR TOBY Now will not I deliver his letter. For the behaviour of the young gentleman gives him out to be of good capacity and breeding; his employment between his lord and my niece confirms no less. Therefore this letter, being so excellently ignorant, will breed no terror in the youth; he will find it comes from a clodpole. But, sir, I will deliver his challenge by word of mouth; set upon Aguecheek a notable report of valour, and drive the gentleman – as I know his youth will aptly receive it

190 – into a most hideous opinion of his rage, skill, fury, and impetuosity. This will so fright them both, that they will kill one another by the look, like cockatrices.

Enter Olivia and Viola

FABIAN Here he comes with your niece. Give them way till he take leave, and presently after him.

SIR TOBY I will meditate the while upon some horrid message for a challenge.

Exit Maria

Sir Toby and Fabian stand aside

OLIVIA

I have said too much unto a heart of stone,
And laid mine honour too unchary on't.
There's something in me that reproves my fault.
But such a headstrong, potent fault it is, 200
That it but mocks reproof.

VIOLA

With the same 'haviour that your passion bears
Goes on my master's griefs.

OLIVIA

Here, wear this jewel for me, 'tis my picture.
Refuse it not, it hath no tongue to vex you.
And, I beseech you, come again tomorrow.
What shall you ask of me that I'll deny,
That honour saved may upon asking give?

VIOLA

Nothing but this: your true love for my master.

OLIVIA

How with mine honour may I give him that 210
Which I have given to you?

VIOLA I will acquit you.

OLIVIA

Well, come again tomorrow. Fare thee well.
A fiend like thee might bear my soul to hell. *Exit*

Sir Toby and Fabian come forward

SIR TOBY Gentleman, God save thee!

VIOLA And you, sir.

SIR TOBY That defence thou hast, betake thee to't. Of what nature the wrongs are thou hast done him, I know not; but thy intercepter, full of despite, bloody as the hunter, attends thee at the orchard end. Dismount thy tuck; be yare in thy preparation; for thy assailant is 220 quick, skilful, and deadly.

VIOLA You mistake, sir. I am sure no man hath any

quarrel to me. My remembrance is very free and clear from any image of offence done to any man.

SIR TOBY You'll find it otherwise, I assure you. Therefore, if you hold your life at any price, betake you to your guard; for your opposite hath in him what youth, strength, skill, and wrath can furnish man withal.

VIOLA I pray you, sir, what is he?

230 SIR TOBY He is knight dubbed with unhatched rapier and on carpet consideration – but he is a devil in private brawl. Souls and bodies hath he divorced three; and his incensement at this moment is so implacable, that satisfaction can be none, but by pangs of death, and sepulchre. Hob, nob! is his word: give't or take't.

VIOLA I will return again into the house and desire some conduct of the lady. I am no fighter. I have heard of some kind of men that put quarrels purposely on others to taste their valour. Belike this is a man of that quirk.

240 SIR TOBY Sir, no. His indignation derives itself out of a very computent injury. Therefore, get you on and give him his desire. Back you shall not to the house, unless you undertake that with me, which with as much safety you might answer him. Therefore on, or strip your sword stark naked; for meddle you must, that's certain, or forswear to wear iron about you.

VIOLA This is as uncivil as strange. I beseech you, do me this courteous office, as to know of the knight what my offence to him is. It is something of my negligence,

250 nothing of my purpose.

SIR TOBY I will do so. Signor Fabian, stay you by this gentleman till my return. *Exit*

VIOLA Pray you, sir, do you know of this matter?

FABIAN I know the knight is incensed against you, even to a mortal arbitrement, but nothing of the circumstance more.

VIOLA I beseech you, what manner of man is he?

FABIAN Nothing of that wonderful promise, to read him by his form, as you are like to find him in the proof of his valour. He is indeed, sir, the most skilful, bloody, 260 and fatal opposite that you could possibly have found in any part of Illyria. Will you walk towards him? I will make your peace with him, if I can.

VIOLA I shall be much bound to you for't. I am one that had rather go with Sir Priest than Sir Knight; I care not who knows so much of my mettle.

Enter Sir Toby and Sir Andrew

SIR TOBY Why, man, he's a very devil. I have not seen such a firago. I had a pass with him, rapier, scabbard and all; and he gives me the stuck-in with such a mortal motion that it is inevitable; and on the answer, he pays 270 you as surely as your feet hits the ground they step on. They say he has been fencer to the Sophy.

SIR ANDREW Pox on't! I'll not meddle with him.

SIR TOBY Ay, but he will not now be pacified. Fabian can scarce hold him yonder.

SIR ANDREW Plague on't! An I thought he had been valiant, and so cunning in fence, I'd have seen him damned ere I'd have challenged him. Let him let the matter slip, and I'll give him my horse, grey Capilet.

SIR TOBY I'll make the motion. Stand here, make a good 280 show on't. This shall end without the perdition of souls. *(Aside, as he crosses to Fabian)* Marry, I'll ride your horse as well as I ride you! *(To Fabian)* I have his horse to take up the quarrel. I have persuaded him the youth's a devil.

FABIAN He is as horribly conceited of him, and pants and looks pale as if a bear were at his heels.

SIR TOBY (*to Viola*) There's no remedy, sir, he will fight with you for's oath's sake. Marry, he hath better be-

290 thought him of his quarrel, and he finds that now scarce to be worth talking of. Therefore, draw for the supportance of his vow. He protests he will not hurt you.

VIOLA (*aside*) Pray God defend me! A little thing would make me tell them how much I lack of a man.

FABIAN Give ground if you see him furious.

SIR TOBY (*crossing to Sir Andrew*) Come, Sir Andrew, there's no remedy. The gentleman will, for his honour's sake, have one bout with you, he cannot by the *duello* avoid it. But he has promised me, as he is a gentleman

300 and a soldier, he will not hurt you. Come on, to't!

SIR ANDREW Pray God he keep his oath!

He draws

Enter Antonio

VIOLA I do assure you, 'tis against my will.

She draws

ANTONIO

Put up your sword. If this young gentleman
Have done offence, I take the fault on me.
If you offend him, I for him defy you.

SIR TOBY You, sir? Why, what are you?

ANTONIO

One, sir, that for his love dares yet do more
Than you have heard him brag to you he will.

SIR TOBY Nay, if you be an undertaker, I am for you.

Enter Officers

310 FABIAN O good Sir Toby, hold! Here come the Officers.

SIR TOBY (*to Antonio*) I'll be with you anon.

VIOLA (*to Sir Andrew*) Pray sir, put your sword up, if you please.

SIR ANDREW Marry, will I, sir. And for that I promised you, I'll be as good as my word. He will bear you easily, and reins well.

FIRST OFFICER This is the man; do thy office.

SECOND OFFICER
Antonio, I arrest thee at the suit
Of Count Orsino.

ANTONIO You do mistake me, sir.

FIRST OFFICER
No, sir, no jot. I know your favour well, 320
Though now you have no sea-cap on your head.
Take him away; he knows I know him well.

ANTONIO
I must obey. *(To Viola)* This comes with seeking you.
But there's no remedy, I shall answer it.
What will you do, now my necessity
Makes me to ask you for my purse? It grieves me
Much more for what I cannot do for you
Than what befalls myself. You stand amazed;
But be of comfort.

SECOND OFFICER Come, sir, away!

ANTONIO I must entreat of you some of that money. 330

VIOLA
What money, sir?
For the fair kindness you have showed me here,
And part being prompted by your present trouble,
Out of my lean and low ability,
I'll lend you something. My having is not much.
I'll make division of my present with you.
Hold: there's half my coffer.

ANTONIO
Will you deny me now?
Is't possible that my deserts to you
Can lack persuasion? Do not tempt my misery, 340
Lest that it make me so unsound a man
As to upbraid you with those kindnesses
That I have done for you.

VIOLA I know of none.

Nor know I you by voice or any feature.
I hate ingratitude more in a man
Than lying, vainness, babbling drunkenness,
Or any taint of vice whose strong corruption
Inhabits our frail blood –

ANTONIO O heavens themselves!

SECOND OFFICER
Come, sir, I pray you go.

ANTONIO
350 Let me speak a little. This youth that you see here
I snatched one half out of the jaws of death;
Relieved him with such sanctity of love;
And to his image, which methought did promise
Most venerable worth, did I devotion.

FIRST OFFICER
What's that to us? The time goes by. Away!

ANTONIO
But O, how vild an idol proves this god!
Thou hast, Sebastian, done good feature shame.
In nature, there's no blemish but the mind;
None can be called deformed, but the unkind.
360 Virtue is beauty; but the beauteous evil
Are empty trunks o'er-flourished by the devil.

FIRST OFFICER
The man grows mad; away with him. Come, come, sir.

ANTONIO
Lead me on. *Exeunt Antonio and Officers*

VIOLA (*aside*)
Methinks his words do from such passion fly
That he believes himself; so do not I?
Prove true, imagination, O, prove true –
That I, dear brother, be now ta'en for you!

SIR TOBY Come hither, knight; come hither, Fabian.
We'll whisper o'er a couplet or two of most sage saws.

VIOLA
He named Sebastian. I my brother know 370
Yet living in my glass. Even such and so
In favour was my brother; and he went
Still in this fashion, colour, ornament,
For him I imitate. O, if it prove,
Tempests are kind, and salt waves fresh in love! *Exit*

SIR TOBY A very dishonest, paltry boy, and more a coward than a hare. His dishonesty appears in leaving his friend here in necessity and denying him; and for his cowardship, ask Fabian.

FABIAN A coward, a most devout coward, religious in it! 380

SIR ANDREW 'Slid! I'll after him again and beat him.

SIR TOBY Do, cuff him soundly, but never draw thy sword.

SIR ANDREW An I do not – *Exit*

FABIAN Come, let's see the event.

SIR TOBY I dare lay any money, 'twill be nothing yet. *Exeunt*

*

Enter Sebastian and Feste IV.1

FESTE Will you make me believe that I am not sent for you?

SEBASTIAN Go to, go to, thou art a foolish fellow. Let me be clear of thee.

FESTE Well held out, i'faith. No: I do not know you; nor I am not sent to you by my lady, to bid you come speak with her; nor your name is not Master Cesario; nor this is not my nose, neither. Nothing that is so, is so.

SEBASTIAN I prithee, vent thy folly somewhere else; thou knowest not me. 10

FESTE Vent my folly! He has heard that word of some great man, and now applies it to a fool. Vent my folly!

I am afraid this great lubber the world will prove a cockney. I prithee now, ungird thy strangeness, and tell me what I shall vent to my lady? Shall I vent to her that thou art coming?

SEBASTIAN I prithee, foolish Greek, depart from me. There's money for thee; if you tarry longer, I shall give worse payment.

20 FESTE By my troth, thou hast an open hand! These wise men that give fools money get themselves a good report – after fourteen years' purchase.

Enter Sir Andrew, Sir Toby, and Fabian

SIR ANDREW Now, sir, have I met you again? There's for you!

He strikes Sebastian

SEBASTIAN Why, there's for thee! And there!

He beats Sir Andrew with the handle of his dagger

And there! Are all the people mad?

SIR TOBY Hold, sir, or I'll throw your dagger o'er the house.

FESTE This will I tell my lady straight. I would not be in
30 some of your coats, for twopence. *Exit*

SIR TOBY Come on, sir, hold!

He grips Sebastian

SIR ANDREW Nay, let him alone. I'll go another way to work with him. I'll have an action of battery against him, if there be any law in Illyria – though I struck him first, yet it's no matter for that.

SEBASTIAN Let go thy hand!

SIR TOBY Come, sir, I will not let you go. Come, my young soldier, put up your iron; you are well fleshed. Come on!

SEBASTIAN
40 I will be free from thee!

He breaks free and draws his sword

What wouldst thou now?

If thou darest tempt me further, draw thy sword.

SIR TOBY What, what! Nay, then, I must have an ounce or two of this malapert blood from you.

He draws

Enter Olivia

OLIVIA

Hold, Toby! On thy life, I charge thee hold!

SIR TOBY Madam!

OLIVIA

Will it be ever thus? Ungracious wretch,
Fit for the mountains and the barbarous caves
Where manners ne'er were preached, out of my sight!
Be not offended, dear Cesario.
Rudesby, be gone! 50

Exeunt Sir Toby, Sir Andrew, and Fabian

I prithee, gentle friend,
Let thy fair wisdom, not thy passion, sway
In this uncivil and unjust extent
Against thy peace. Go with me to my house,
And hear thou there how many fruitless pranks
This ruffian hath botched up, that thou thereby
Mayst smile at this. Thou shalt not choose but go;
Do not deny. Beshrew his soul for me!
He started one poor heart of mine, in thee.

SEBASTIAN (*aside*)

What relish is in this? How runs the stream?
Or I am mad, or else this is a dream. 60
Let fancy still my sense in Lethe steep;
If it be thus to dream, still let me sleep!

OLIVIA

Nay, come, I prithee. Would thou'dst be ruled by me!

SEBASTIAN

Madam, I will.

OLIVIA O, say so, and so be! *Exeunt*

Enter Maria and Feste

MARIA Nay, I prithee, put on this gown and this beard; make him believe thou art Sir Topas the curate. Do it quickly. I'll call Sir Toby the whilst. *Exit*

FESTE Well, I'll put it on and I will dissemble myself in't, and I would I were the first that ever dissembled in such a gown. I am not tall enough to become the function well, nor lean enough to be thought a good student. But to be said an honest man and a good housekeeper goes as fairly as to say a careful man and a great scholar. The
10 competitors enter.

Enter Sir Toby and Maria

SIR TOBY Jove bless thee, Master Parson!

FESTE *Bonos dies*, Sir Toby; for as the old hermit of Prague that never saw pen and ink very wittily said to a niece of King Gorboduc: that that is, is. So I, being Master Parson, am Master Parson; for what is 'that' but 'that'? And 'is' but 'is'?

SIR TOBY To him, Sir Topas.

FESTE What ho, I say! Peace in this prison!

SIR TOBY The knave counterfeits well; a good knave.

20 MALVOLIO (*within*) Who calls there?

FESTE Sir Topas the curate, who comes to visit Malvolio the lunatic.

MALVOLIO Sir Topas, Sir Topas, good Sir Topas, go to my lady –

FESTE Out, hyperbolical fiend, how vexest thou this man! Talkest thou nothing but of ladies?

SIR TOBY Well said, Master Parson.

MALVOLIO Sir Topas, never was man thus wronged. Good Sir Topas, do not think I am mad. They have laid
30 me here in hideous darkness –

FESTE Fie, thou dishonest Satan! I call thee by the most modest terms, for I am one of those gentle ones that will use the devil himself with courtesy. Sayst thou that house is dark?

MALVOLIO As hell, Sir Topas.

FESTE Why, it hath bay windows transparent as barricadoes, and the clerestories toward the south–north are as lustrous as ebony. And yet complainest thou of obstruction!

MALVOLIO I am not mad, Sir Topas. I say to you, this house is dark. 40

FESTE Madman, thou errest. I say there is no darkness but ignorance, in which thou art more puzzled than the Egyptians in their fog.

MALVOLIO I say this house is as dark as ignorance, though ignorance were as dark as hell. And I say there was never man thus abused. I am no more mad than you are – make the trial of it in any constant question.

FESTE What is the opinion of Pythagoras concerning wildfowl? 50

MALVOLIO That the soul of our grandam might haply inhabit a bird.

FESTE What thinkest thou of his opinion?

MALVOLIO I think nobly of the soul, and no way approve his opinion.

FESTE Fare thee well; remain thou still in darkness. Thou shalt hold the opinion of Pythagoras ere I will allow of thy wits, and fear to kill a woodcock lest thou dispossess the soul of thy grandam. Fare thee well.

MALVOLIO Sir Topas, Sir Topas! 60

SIR TOBY My most exquisite Sir Topas!

FESTE Nay, I am for all waters.

MARIA Thou mightst have done this without thy beard and gown; he sees thee not.

SIR TOBY To him in thine own voice, and bring me word how thou findest him. I would we were well rid of this knavery. If he may be conveniently delivered, I would he were, for I am now so far in offence with my niece that I cannot pursue with any safety this sport the upshot. Come by and by to my chamber. 70

Exeunt Sir Toby and Maria

FESTE (*sings*)

Hey Robin, jolly Robin!
Tell me how thy lady does –

MALVOLIO Fool!

FESTE (*sings*)

My lady is unkind, perdy.

MALVOLIO Fool!

FESTE (*sings*)

Alas, why is she so?

MALVOLIO Fool, I say!

FESTE (*sings*)

She loves another –

Who calls, ha?

80 MALVOLIO Good fool, as ever thou wilt deserve well at my hand, help me to a candle, and pen, ink, and paper. As I am a gentleman, I will live to be thankful to thee for't.

FESTE Master Malvolio?

MALVOLIO Ay, good fool.

FESTE Alas, sir, how fell you besides your five wits?

MALVOLIO Fool, there was never man so notoriously abused. I am as well in my wits, fool, as thou art.

FESTE But as well? Then you are mad indeed, if you be no better in your wits than a fool. 90

MALVOLIO They have here propertied me; keep me in darkness, send ministers to me – asses! – and do all they can to face me out of my wits.

FESTE Advise you what you say. The minister is here. *(In priest's voice)* Malvolio, Malvolio, thy wits the heavens restore! Endeavour thyself to sleep and leave thy vain bibble-babble.

MALVOLIO Sir Topas!

FESTE Maintain no words with him, good fellow. *(In own voice)* Who, I, sir? Not I, sir! God buy you, good Sir Topas! *(In priest's voice)* Marry, amen! *(In own voice)* I will, sir, I will. 100

MALVOLIO Fool! Fool! Fool, I say!

FESTE Alas, sir, be patient. What say you sir? I am shent for speaking to you.

MALVOLIO Good fool, help me to some light and some paper. I tell thee, I am as well in my wits as any man in Illyria.

FESTE Well-a-day, that you were, sir!

MALVOLIO By this hand, I am! Good fool, some ink, paper, and light; and convey what I will set down to my lady. It shall advantage thee more than ever the bearing of letter did. 110

FESTE I will help you to't. But tell me true, are you not mad indeed, or do you but counterfeit?

MALVOLIO Believe me, I am not. I tell thee true.

FESTE Nay, I'll ne'er believe a madman till I see his brains. I will fetch you light, and paper, and ink.

MALVOLIO Fool, I'll requite it in the highest degree. I prithee, be gone. 120

FESTE (*sings*)

I am gone, sir, and anon, sir,
  I'll be with you again.
In a trice, like to the old Vice,
  Your need to sustain.
Who with dagger of lath, in his rage and his wrath,
  Cries 'Ah ha!' to the devil;
Like a mad lad – 'Pare thy nails, dad?
  Adieu, goodman devil!' *Exit*

IV.3 *Enter Sebastian*

SEBASTIAN

This is the air; that is the glorious sun;
This pearl she gave me, I do feel't and see't;
And though 'tis wonder that enwraps me thus,
Yet 'tis not madness. Where's Antonio, then?
I could not find him at the Elephant.
Yet there he was; and there I found this credit
That he did range the town to seek me out.
His counsel now might do me golden service.
For though my soul disputes well with my sense
10 That this may be some error, but no madness,
Yet doth this accident and flood of fortune
So far exceed all instance, all discourse,
That I am ready to distrust mine eyes,
And wrangle with my reason that persuades me
To any other trust but that I am mad –
Or else the lady's mad; yet if 'twere so,
She could not sway her house, command her followers,
Take and give back affairs and their dispatch,
With such a smooth, discreet, and stable bearing
20 As I perceive she does. There's something in't
That is deceivable. But here the lady comes.

Enter Olivia and a Priest

OLIVIA

Blame not this haste of mine. If you mean well,
Now go with me and with this holy man
Into the chantry by; there before him
And underneath that consecrated roof
Plight me the full assurance of your faith,
That my most jealous and too doubtful soul
May live at peace. He shall conceal it
Whiles you are willing it shall come to note;
30 What time we will our celebration keep

According to my birth. What do you say?

SEBASTIAN

I'll follow this good man, and go with you;
And having sworn truth, ever will be true.

OLIVIA

Then lead the way, good father, and heavens so shine
That they may fairly note this act of mine!

Exeunt

*

Enter Feste and Fabian V.1

FABIAN Now, as thou lov'st me, let me see his letter.

FESTE Good Master Fabian, grant me another request.

FABIAN Anything!

FESTE Do not desire to see this letter.

FABIAN This is to give a dog, and in recompense desire my dog again.

Enter Orsino, Viola, Curio, and lords

ORSINO Belong you to the Lady Olivia, friends?

FESTE Ay, sir, we are some of her trappings.

ORSINO I know thee well. How dost thou, my good fellow? 10

FESTE Truly, sir, the better for my foes, and the worse for my friends.

ORSINO Just the contrary: the better for thy friends.

FESTE No, sir: the worse.

ORSINO How can that be?

FESTE Marry, sir, they praise me – and make an ass of me. Now my foes tell me plainly, I am an ass; so that by my foes, sir, I profit in the knowledge of myself, and by my friends I am abused. So that, conclusions to be as kisses, if your four negatives make your two affirma- 20 tives, why then, the worse for my friends and the better for my foes.

ORSINO Why, this is excellent.

FESTE By my troth, sir, no – though it please you to be one of my friends.

ORSINO Thou shalt not be the worse for me: there's gold.

FESTE But that it would be double-dealing, sir, I would you could make it another.

ORSINO O, you give me ill counsel!

30 FESTE Put your grace in your pocket, sir, for this once, and let your flesh and blood obey it.

ORSINO Well, I will be so much a sinner to be a double-dealer; there's another.

FESTE *Primo, secundo, tertio*, is a good play; and the old saying is, the third pays for all; the triplex, sir, is a good tripping measure; or the bells of Saint Bennet, sir, may put you in mind – one, two, three!

ORSINO You can fool no more money out of me at this throw. If you will let your lady know I am here to speak
40 with her, and bring her along with you, it may awake my bounty further.

FESTE Marry, sir, lullaby to your bounty till I come again. I go, sir, but I would not have you to think that my desire of having is the sin of covetousness. But as you say, sir, let your bounty take a nap – I will awake it anon. *Exit*

Enter Antonio and Officers

VIOLA
Here comes the man, sir, that did rescue me.

ORSINO
That face of his I do remember well.
Yet when I saw it last, it was besmeared
50 As black as Vulcan in the smoke of war.
A baubling vessel was he captain of,

For shallow draught and bulk, unprizable;
With which, such scatheful grapple did he make
With the most noble bottom of our fleet,
That very envy and the tongue of loss
Cried fame and honour on him. What's the matter?

FIRST OFFICER

Orsino, this is that Antonio
That took the *Phoenix*, and her fraught from Candy;
And this is he that did the *Tiger* board
When your young nephew Titus lost his leg. 60
Here in the streets, desperate of shame and state,
In private brabble did we apprehend him.

VIOLA

He did me kindness, sir, drew on my side,
But in conclusion put strange speech upon me.
I know not what 'twas, but distraction.

ORSINO

Notable pirate, thou salt-water thief,
What foolish boldness brought thee to their mercies
Whom thou, in terms so bloody and so dear,
Hast made thine enemies?

ANTONIO

Orsino, noble sir, 70
Be pleased that I shake off these names you give me.
Antonio never yet was thief or pirate;
Though, I confess, on base and ground enough,
Orsino's enemy. A witchcraft drew me hither.
That most ingrateful boy there by your side
From the rude sea's enraged and foamy mouth
Did I redeem; a wrack past hope he was.
His life I gave him, and did thereto add
My love without retention or restraint,
All his in dedication. For his sake 80
Did I expose myself – pure for his love –

Into the danger of this adverse town;
Drew to defend him when he was beset;
Where, being apprehended, his false cunning –
Not meaning to partake with me in danger –
Taught him to face me out of his acquaintance,
And grew a twenty years' removèd thing
While one would wink; denied me mine own purse
Which I had recommended to his use
90 Not half an hour before.

VIOLA How can this be?

ORSINO
When came he to this town?

ANTONIO
Today, my lord; and for three months before
No interim, not a minute's vacancy,
Both day and night, did we keep company.

Enter Olivia and attendants

ORSINO
Here comes the Countess; now heaven walks on earth!
But for thee, fellow – fellow, thy words are madness.
Three months this youth hath tended upon me.
But more of that anon. Take him aside.

OLIVIA
What would my lord – but that he may not have –
100 Wherein Olivia may seem serviceable?
Cesario, you do not keep promise with me.

VIOLA
Madam?

ORSINO
Gracious Olivia –

OLIVIA
What do you say, Cesario? *(To Orsino)* Good, my lord.

VIOLA
My lord would speak; my duty hushes me.

OLIVIA

If it be aught to the old tune, my lord,
It is as fat and fulsome to mine ear
As howling after music.

ORSINO

Still so cruel?

OLIVIA Still so constant, lord.

ORSINO

What, to perverseness? You uncivil lady, 110
To whose ingrate and unauspicious altars
My soul the faithfull'st offerings have breathed out
That e'er devotion tendered! What shall I do?

OLIVIA

Even what it please my lord, that shall become him.

ORSINO

Why should I not – had I the heart to do it –
Like to th'Egyptian thief at point of death
Kill what I love – a savage jealousy
That sometime savours nobly? But hear me this:
Since you to non-regardance cast my faith,
And that I partly know the instrument 120
That screws me from my true place in your favour,
Live you the marble-breasted tyrant still.
But this your minion, whom I know you love,
And whom, by heaven, I swear, I tender dearly,
Him will I tear out of that cruel eye
Where he sits crownèd in his master's spite.
Come, boy, with me, my thoughts are ripe in mischief.
I'll sacrifice the lamb that I do love
To spite a raven's heart within a dove.

VIOLA

And I, most jocund, apt, and willingly 130
To do you rest, a thousand deaths would die.

OLIVIA

Where goes Cesario?

VIOLA After him I love

More than I love these eyes, more than my life,
More by all mores than e'er I shall love wife.
If I do feign, you witnesses above,
Punish my life, for tainting of my love!

OLIVIA

Ay me, detested! How am I beguiled!

VIOLA

Who does beguile you? Who does do you wrong?

OLIVIA

Hast thou forgot thyself? Is it so long?
140 Call forth the holy father! *Exit an attendant*

ORSINO Come, away!

OLIVIA

Whither, my lord? Cesario, husband, stay!

ORSINO

Husband?

OLIVIA Ay, husband. Can he that deny?

ORSINO

Her husband, sirrah?

VIOLA No, my lord, not I.

OLIVIA

Alas, it is the baseness of thy fear
That makes thee strangle thy propriety.
Fear not, Cesario, take thy fortunes up.
Be that thou know'st thou art, and then thou art
As great as that thou fear'st.

Enter Priest

O, welcome, Father.

Father, I charge thee, by thy reverence,
150 Here to unfold – though lately we intended
To keep in darkness what occasion now

Reveals before 'tis ripe – what thou dost know
Hath newly passed between this youth and me.

PRIEST
A contract of eternal bond of love,
Confirmed by mutual joinder of your hands,
Attested by the holy close of lips,
Strengthened by interchangement of your rings,
And all the ceremony of this compact
Sealed in my function, by my testimony;
Since when, my watch hath told me, toward my grave 160
I have travelled but two hours.

ORSINO
O thou dissembling cub! What wilt thou be
When time hath sowed a grizzle on thy case?
Or will not else thy craft so quickly grow
That thine own trip shall be thine overthrow?
Farewell, and take her; but direct thy feet
Where thou and I henceforth may never meet.

VIOLA
My lord, I do protest –

OLIVIA O, do not swear!
Hold little faith, though thou hast too much fear.

Enter Sir Andrew

SIR ANDREW For the love of God, a surgeon! Send one 170
presently to Sir Toby.

OLIVIA What's the matter?

SIR ANDREW He's broke my head across, and he's given
Sir Toby a bloody coxcomb too. For the love of God,
your help! I had rather than forty pound I were at home.

OLIVIA Who has done this, Sir Andrew?

SIR ANDREW The Count's gentleman, one Cesario. We
took him for a coward, but he's the very devil incardinate.

ORSINO My gentleman, Cesario? 180

SIR ANDREW 'Od's lifelings, here he is! You broke my head for nothing; and that that I did, I was set on to do't by Sir Toby.

VIOLA
Why do you speak to me? I never hurt you.
You drew your sword upon me without cause,
But I bespake you fair, and hurt you not.

Enter Sir Toby and Feste

SIR ANDREW If a bloody coxcomb be a hurt, you have hurt me. I think you set nothing by a bloody coxcomb. Here comes Sir Toby halting, you shall hear more; but 190 if he had not been in drink, he would have tickled you othergates than he did.

ORSINO How now, gentleman? How is't with you?

SIR TOBY That's all one; he's hurt me, and there's the end on't. *(To Feste)* Sot, didst see Dick Surgeon, sot?

FESTE O, he's drunk, Sir Toby, an hour agone. His eyes were set at eight i'the morning.

SIR TOBY Then he's a rogue and a passy-measures pavin. I hate a drunken rogue.

OLIVIA Away with him! Who hath made this havoc with 200 them?

SIR ANDREW I'll help you, Sir Toby, because we'll be dressed together.

SIR TOBY Will you help? An asshead, and a coxcomb, and a knave – a thin-faced knave, a gull!

OLIVIA Get him to bed, and let his hurt be looked to.

Exeunt Sir Toby and Sir Andrew,
helped by Feste and Fabian

Enter Sebastian

SEBASTIAN
I am sorry, madam, I have hurt your kinsman.
But had it been the brother of my blood
I must have done no less, with wit and safety.

You throw a strange regard upon me; and by that
I do perceive it hath offended you. 210
Pardon me, sweet one, even for the vows
We made each other but so late ago.

ORSINO

One face, one voice, one habit, and two persons!
A natural perspective, that is and is not.

SEBASTIAN

Antonio! O, my dear Antonio!
How have the hours racked and tortured me
Since I have lost thee!

ANTONIO

Sebastian, are you?

SEBASTIAN Fear'st thou that, Antonio?

ANTONIO

How have you made division of yourself?
An apple cleft in two is not more twin 220
Than these two creatures. Which is Sebastian?

OLIVIA

Most wonderful!

SEBASTIAN

Do I stand there? I never had a brother;
Nor can there be that deity in my nature
Of here and everywhere. I had a sister
Whom the blind waves and surges have devoured.
Of charity, what kin are you to me?
What countryman? What name? What parentage?

VIOLA

Of Messaline. Sebastian was my father.
Such a Sebastian was my brother too. 230
So went he suited to his watery tomb.
If spirits can assume both form and suit
You come to fright us.

SEBASTIAN A spirit I am indeed,

But am in that dimension grossly clad
Which from the womb I did participate.
Were you a woman, as the rest goes even,
I should my tears let fall upon your cheek,
And say, 'Thrice welcome, drownèd Viola.'

VIOLA

My father had a mole upon his brow.

SEBASTIAN

240 And so had mine.

VIOLA

And died that day when Viola from her birth
Had numbered thirteen years.

SEBASTIAN

O, that record is lively in my soul.
He finishèd indeed his mortal act
That day that made my sister thirteen years.

VIOLA

If nothing lets to make us happy both
But this my masculine usurped attire,
Do not embrace me, till each circumstance
Of place, time, fortune, do cohere and jump
250 That I am Viola; which to confirm,
I'll bring you to a captain in this town
Where lie my maiden weeds; by whose gentle help
I was preserved to serve this noble Count.
All the occurrence of my fortune since
Hath been between this lady and this lord.

SEBASTIAN (*to Olivia*)

So comes it, lady, you have been mistook.
But nature to her bias drew in that.
You would have been contracted to a maid.
Nor are you therein, by my life, deceived:
260 You are betrothed both to a maid and man.

ORSINO

Be not amazed; right noble is his blood.
If this be so, as yet the glass seems true,
I shall have share in this most happy wrack.
(To Viola) Boy, thou hast said to me a thousand times
Thou never shouldst love woman like to me.

VIOLA

And all those sayings will I overswear
And all those swearings keep as true in soul
As doth that orbèd continent the fire
That severs day from night.

ORSINO Give me thy hand,
And let me see thee in thy woman's weeds. 270

VIOLA

The Captain that did bring me first on shore
Hath my maid's garments. He, upon some action,
Is now in durance at Malvolio's suit,
A gentleman and follower of my lady's.

OLIVIA

He shall enlarge him; fetch Malvolio hither.
And yet, alas, now I remember me,
They say, poor gentleman, he's much distract.

Enter Feste with a letter, and Fabian

A most extracting frenzy of mine own
From my remembrance clearly banished his.
(To Feste) How does he, sirrah? 280

FESTE Truly, madam, he holds Beelzebub at the stave's end as well as a man in his case may do. He's here writ a letter to you. I should have given it you today morning. But as a madman's epistles are no gospels, so it skills not much when they are delivered.

OLIVIA Open it, and read it.

FESTE Look, then, to be well edified when the fool delivers the madman.

He reads frantically

By the Lord, madam –

290 OLIVIA How now, art thou mad?

FESTE No, madam; I do but read madness. An your ladyship will have it as it ought to be, you must allow *vox*.

OLIVIA Prithee, read i'thy right wits.

FESTE So I do, madonna; but to read his right wits, is to read thus. Therefore, perpend, my princess, and give ear.

OLIVIA (*snatching the letter and giving it to Fabian*) Read it you, sirrah.

FABIAN (*reads*)

300 *By the Lord, madam, you wrong me, and the world shall know it. Though you have put me into darkness and given your drunken cousin rule over me, yet have I the benefit of my senses as well as your ladyship. I have your own letter that induced me to the semblance I put on; with the which I doubt not but to do myself much right, or you much shame. Think of me as you please, I leave my duty a little unthought-of, and speak out of my injury. The madly-used Malvolio.*

OLIVIA Did he write this?

310 FESTE Ay, madam.

ORSINO This savours not much of distraction.

OLIVIA

See him delivered, Fabian, bring him hither.

Exit Fabian

My lord, so please you, these things further thought on,
To think me as well a sister as a wife,
One day shall crown th'alliance on't, so please you,

Here at my house, and at my proper cost.

ORSINO

Madam, I am most apt t'embrace your offer.
(To Viola) Your master quits you; and for your service
done him
So much against the mettle of your sex,
So far beneath your soft and tender breeding, 320
And since you called me master for so long,
Here is my hand; you shall from this time be
Your master's mistress.

OLIVIA A sister, you are she.

Enter Malvolio and Fabian

ORSINO

Is this the madman?

OLIVIA Ay, my lord, this same.
How now, Malvolio?

MALVOLIO

Madam, you have done me wrong;
Notorious wrong.

OLIVIA Have I, Malvolio? No!

MALVOLIO

Lady, you have; pray you, peruse that letter.
You must not now deny it is your hand.
Write from it if you can, in hand or phrase, 330
Or say 'tis not your seal, not your invention;
You can say none of this. Well, grant it then,
And tell me in the modesty of honour,
Why you have given me such clear lights of favour?
Bade me come smiling and cross-gartered to you,
To put on yellow stockings, and to frown
Upon Sir Toby and the lighter people?
And, acting this in an obedient hope,
Why have you suffered me to be imprisoned,
Kept in a dark house, visited by the priest, 340

And made the most notorious geck and gull
That e'er invention played on? Tell me why?

OLIVIA
Alas, Malvolio, this is not my writing,
Though, I confess, much like the character.
But out of question 'tis Maria's hand.
And now I do bethink me, it was she
First told me thou wast mad; then, camest in smiling,
And in such forms which here were presupposed
Upon thee in the letter. Prithee, be content.
350 This practice hath most shrewdly passed upon thee;
But when we know the grounds and authors of it,
Thou shalt be both the plaintiff and the judge
Of thine own cause.

FABIAN Good madam, hear me speak;
And let no quarrel, nor no brawl to come,
Taint the condition of this present hour,
Which I have wondered at. In hope it shall not,
Most freely I confess, myself and Toby
Set this device against Malvolio here,
Upon some stubborn and uncourteous parts
360 We had conceived against him. Maria writ
The letter at Sir Toby's great importance,
In recompense whereof, he hath married her.
How with a sportful malice it was followed
May rather pluck on laughter than revenge,
If that the injuries be justly weighed
That have on both sides passed.

OLIVIA
Alas, poor fool! How have they baffled thee!

FESTE Why, 'Some are born great, some achieve greatness, and some have greatness thrown upon them.' I
370 was one, sir, in this interlude, one Sir Topas, sir – but that's all one. 'By the Lord, fool, I am not mad!' But do

you remember: 'Madam, why laugh you at such a barren rascal, an you smile not, he's gagged'? And thus the whirligig of time brings in his revenges.

MALVOLIO

I'll be revenged on the whole pack of you! *Exit*

OLIVIA

He hath been most notoriously abused.

ORSINO

Pursue him and entreat him to a peace.
He hath not told us of the Captain yet.
When that is known, and golden time convents,
A solemn combination shall be made 380
Of our dear souls. Meantime, sweet sister,
We will not part from hence. Cesario, come;
For so you shall be, while you are a man.
But when in other habits you are seen –
Orsino's mistress, and his fancy's queen!

Exeunt all but Feste

FESTE (*sings*)

When that I was and a little tiny boy,
  With hey-ho, the wind and the rain;
A foolish thing was but a toy,
  For the rain it raineth every day.

But when I came to man's estate, 390
  With hey-ho, the wind and the rain;
'Gainst knaves and thieves men shut their gate,
  For the rain it raineth every day.

But when I came, alas, to wive,
  With hey-ho, the wind and the rain;
By swaggering could I never thrive,
  For the rain it raineth every day.

But when I came unto my beds,
  With hey-ho, the wind and the rain;

400 With tosspots still had drunken heads,
For the rain it raineth every day.

A great while ago the world began,
With hey-ho, the wind and the rain;
But that's all one, our play is done,
And we'll strive to please you every day. *Exit*

COMMENTARY

REFERENCES to plays by Shakespeare not yet available in the New Penguin Shakespeare are to Peter Alexander's edition of the *Complete Works*, London, 1951. 'Folio' (F) means the first collected edition of Shakespeare's plays, published in 1623.

The title

The original spelling of the title, *Twelfe Night*, preserves the form of the ordinal number which was common in Shakespeare's day.

I.1 The eighteenth-century custom of localizing scenes ('A street', etc.) has been dropped in this edition. Shakespeare's audience was interested in the relation of characters to one another, not in their relation to any particular place, except when the place itself was part of the action. *Twelfth Night* could have been acted on a very simple stage in a great hall, or perhaps even in the floor space in front of the two big doorways at the screen end of such a hall. These doorways would soon establish themselves as leading to Olivia's house and to Orsino's, and the strangers to the town would arrive by a third entrance, perhaps through the audience. The doors or the curtained doorways could also serve for the box-tree and for the dark house (see Introduction, page 8) or these could be brought on as two substantial properties. The only other requirements would be two or three easily movable seats. No upper stage is needed. When the play was performed at the Globe, the dark house could have been represented by the curtained booth between the two main entrances to the stage.

(stage direction) *Music*. At the original production in a great hall, this music may have been provided by a seated group of performers on the viol and bass viol, who would have been playing to the company before the play started. When the play was repeated in the public theatre, Orsino's own group of musicians, playing portable instruments such as recorders, a lute, and an arch-lute, could enter with him.

(stage direction) *Orsino*. The link which has been suggested between this character and the historical Virginio Orsino, Duke of Bracciano, is discussed in the Introduction, pages 22–24.

3 *appetite* (Orsino's longing for music)

4 *fall* cadence

9–14 *O spirit of love, how quick and fresh art thou . . . in a minute*. The involved syntax of these lines perhaps led either the playhouse copyist or the compositor to insert a full stop after 'sea' in line 11, but this does not give good sense unless we read 'Receivest' for 'Receiveth'. The general meaning is clear: love is so ravenous that nothing it devours can give it real satisfaction.

9 *quick and fresh* keen and eager (to devour or consume)

12 *validity* value

pitch (1) height; (2) excellence

13 *abatement* depreciation

15 *alone* exceeding all other passions

high fantastical intensely imaginative. 'Fantastical' was a fashionable bit of psychological jargon.

19 *Why, so I do*. Orsino's pun on 'heart' and 'hart' betrays his lordly possessiveness; he thinks he should command where he adores.

23–4 *And my desires, like fell and cruel hounds, | E'er since pursue me*. Orsino recalls a classical legend which Shakespeare would know best from Ovid's *Metamorphoses* (iii. 138 onwards): the hunter Actaeon, because he saw the goddess Diana naked, was turned into a stag and torn to pieces by his hounds.

23 *fell* savage

27 *element* sky

heat. This is often emended to 'hence', but *heat* suggests the way the passage of the seasons will destroy Olivia's beauty, if she spends the best years of her life in mourning.

29 *a cloistress* an enclosed nun

31 *eye-offending brine* stinging tears

season preserve by salting

33 *remembrance* (pronounced as four syllables)

34 *frame* construction

36 *shaft* arrow (shot by Cupid)

38 *liver, brain, and heart* (the seats of the passions, judgement, and sentiments)

40 *Her sweet perfections*. Olivia's nature will be completed by Orsino's occupying each of these thrones. The condescension is in character, but the idea that 'woman receiveth perfection by the man' is common in the period.

self sole

I.2 (stage direction) *Viola*. This name probably derives, without Shakespeare being fully aware of the fact, from a romance published in 1598: *The Famous History of Parismus*, by Emanuel Forde. It is set in Thessaly, a country ruled by Queen Olivia. The heroine Violetta disguises as a page and seeks service with the man she loves. But apart from this girl-page theme, *Parismus* had little to interest Shakespeare.

2 *Illyria*. This name for what is now Yugoslavia conjures up the world of late Greek romances, but the local colour of the play is all English.

4 *Elysium* (abode of the happy dead, hence heaven)

6, 7 *perchance.* The Captain and Viola play on the meanings 'perhaps' and 'by good fortune'.

8 *chance* what may have happened

11 *driving* drifting

14 *lived* kept afloat (a nautical term)

15 *Arion.* This was the name of a Greek musician who threw himself overboard to escape being murdered by sailors, and was carried to land by a dolphin which had heard him play on the ship. Ovid tells the legend in the *Fasti*, II, 79–118.

16 *hold acquaintance with the waves* 'bob up and down as if greeting the waves' or perhaps 'follow every movement of the waves'

19–21 *Mine own escape unfoldeth to my hope | ... The like of him* my own escape encourages me in the hope, which is warranted by what you have just said, that he also has escaped

32 *murmur* rumour

43 *delivered* revealed

45 *estate* status. Viola does not want her true identity to be disclosed until she has decided the time is ripe for it to be known.

compass bring about

46 *suit* petition

49–50 *nature with a beauteous wall | Doth oft close in pollution.* Like the reference to Arion's story in line 15, this may be a vestigial remnant of the sea captain's villainy in Rich's 'Apolonius and Silla' (*Elizabethan Love Stories*, ed. T. J. B. Spencer, pp. 101–3; see Further Reading). It also prepares us for Antonio's bitter reproach of what he takes to be Sebastian's treachery later in the play.

52 *character* appearance and behaviour

55–6 *as haply shall become | The form of my intent* as may be suitable for the purpose I have shaped

58 *I can sing.* For Shakespeare's possible change of plan here, see Introduction, page 20.

60 *allow* prove

62 *wit* design

63 *mute*. Dumb attendants, as well as eunuchs, were known by the Elizabethans to be part of the entourage of oriental monarchs.

3.1 *my niece*. On the strength of this expression, Sir Toby is usually described as Olivia's uncle. Maria and Olivia herself speak of him as Olivia's 'cousin', but this term could be used in Elizabethan English for any collateral relative other than a brother or sister.

3 *By my troth* by my faith (an asseveration)

6 *except before excepted* exclude what has already been excluded (a legal phrase). Sir Toby may mean that Olivia has not taken exception to his 'ill hours' in the past and should not do so now.

8 *modest limits of order* bounds of good behaviour

11 *an* if

18 *tall* courageous. Maria takes the word in its usual sense.
any's any who is

20 *ducats*. A ducat was worth a third of £1.

21 *have but a year in all these ducats*. Maria means Sir Andrew will get through his fortune in a year.

22 *very* perfect

23–4 *viol-de-gamboys* bass viol, or *viol da gamba* (ancestor of the modern violoncello)

25 *without book* by memory

26 *natural* like an idiot or 'natural'

28–30 *gift of a coward . . . gift of a grave* (with a play on the meanings 'natural ability' and 'present')

28 *gust* relish

31–2 *substractors* detractors

37 *coistrel* groom, low fellow. The word does not occur elsewhere in Shakespeare's work, and it has been suggested that he picked it up from Rich's *Farewell to Military Profession*. But it is not uncommon in the period, and still survives in North of England dialects.

39 *parish top.* There are several references to parish tops in Elizabethan plays, but nothing is known about them.

Castiliano, vulgo. This is a puzzling phrase. We would expect it to mean 'Talk of the devil!' (from the proverb 'Talk of the devil and he will appear'), since Sir Toby has just caught sight of Sir Andrew. *Castiliano* is in fact the name adopted by the devil Belphegor when he comes to earth in *Grim the Collier of Croydon, or The Devil and his Dame*, a play written in or before 1600; and Shakespeare may here be alluding to this play in order to give a new twist to an old saying. He would have been reminded of the play in reading Rich's collection of tales, because Rich tells the story on which the play is based – how the devil was worsted by a woman – in his Conclusion. Sir Toby's mention of a parish top also connects the two plays. The scene in *Grim the Collier* which immediately follows Belphegor's assumption of the name Castiliano starts with Grim complaining 'Every night I dream I am a town top.' We would expect '*vulgo*', meaning 'in the common tongue' to be followed by 'devil', but perhaps Sir Toby, warned by the proverb, makes the gesture of horns instead. '*Vulgo*' could also follow the noun to which it referred, and if it does here, Shakespeare, by saying the devil was Castiliano in the common tongue, or to the common people, is commenting on the popularity of the old play.

40 *Agueface.* This form of Sir Andrew's name has led editors to emend '*vulgo*' to '*volto*' and explain that Sir Toby is telling Maria to put on a solemn face like a Castilian, or Spaniard, to suit with Sir Andrew's expression. Shakespeare is often, however, a little uncertain about the form of a character's name near the beginning of a play, and there may be no joke intended.

(stage direction) *Sir Andrew Aguecheek.* This name has been learnedly explained as being from Spanish '*andrajo*', 'a despicable person', or from '*aguicia chica*' meaning 'little wit'. But to Shakespeare's audience it would simply suggest the shaking cheeks of cowardice.

44 *shrew*. This is usually explained as an allusion to Maria's mouse-like size. It could also be another unconscious recollection of *Grim the Collier*, in which the devil's human wife is an untamable shrew called Marian and a waiting-gentlewoman into the bargain.

46 *accost*. Great play is made with the word '*accostare*' in *Gl'Ingannati*, but plays contemporary with *Twelfth Night* show that it was also fashionable in England, in the form 'accost', at the end of the sixteenth century. Like 'board' (line 54), it was a nautical metaphor, meaning 'address' or 'greet'. Sir Andrew takes both words in a more concrete sense than Sir Toby intends.

48 *chambermaid* (not a menial position; more like the modern 'lady companion')

58 *let part so* let her go thus (without ceremony)

62 *in hand* to deal with

64 *Marry* (a mild oath, originally 'By Mary')

66 *Thought is free*. This was the stock retort to 'Do you think I'm a fool?' and is one of many proverbs and stock phrases to do with fools and folly used in this play.

67 *buttery bar* (ledge in front of the hatch through which drink was handed out from the buttery, or store-room for liquor)

70 *It's dry*. Maria means 'thirsty', but hints at a supposed sign of impotence. In *Othello* III.4.38 a moist palm 'argues fruitfulness and liberal heart'.

72 *keep my hand dry* (in allusion to the proverb 'Fools have wit enough to keep themselves dry')

73 *A dry jest*. Maria puns on the meanings 'stupid' and 'mocking, ironic'.

77 *canary* (a sweet wine, originally from the Canary Islands)

78 *put down* defeated in repartee. Sir Andrew plays with the literal meaning.

81 *a Christian* (any normal man)

an ordinary man. Since *Christian* here means 'ordinary'

in the modern sense, *an ordinary man* may mean an eater of court rations. The ordinary was the common table.

82 *eater of beef.* Medical writers of the period argued that beef made men low and melancholy, and 'beef-witted' is an insult in *Troilus and Cressida*, II.1.13.

87 *Pourquoi?* why? (French)

94–5 *curl by nature.* The Folio reads 'coole my nature'. This skilful emendation by the eighteenth-century editor, Theobald, is confirmed by the pun on 'tongues' and 'tongs', which were pronounced alike in Elizabethan English, and by the antithesis between 'art' and 'nature'.

98 *huswife.* The Folio spelling preserves Sir Toby's pun. 'Housewife' (Middle English 'huswif') and 'hussy' had diverged in meaning, but not in pronunciation, at this time. The Elizabethans believed venereal disease and sexual excess to be among the causes of baldness.

109 *kickshawses* trifles (French *quelquechoses*)

111 *betters* social superiors

112 *old man* old hand, someone experienced

113 *galliard.* This was a lively five-step dance in which the fifth step was a leap, or caper. The puns in the next few lines may owe something to the quibbles on dancing terms in the epistle dedicatory in Rich's *Farewell to Military Profession.*

114 *caper.* Sir Toby quibbles on the meaning 'a spice to season mutton'.

116 *back-trick.* Sir Andrew means either the special backward leap called the *riccacciata*, or the reversed series of steps in a galliard; but the audience is meant to catch the sexual meaning of 'trick', following on 'mutton', which could mean 'a loose woman'.

120 *Mistress Mall's picture.* Paintings were frequently protected by curtains. Mistress Mall has been identified as Mary Fitton, a lady-in-waiting who became involved in a court scandal in 1601, and this identification would be

probable if we could be sure that Malvolio is a portrait of Mary Fitton's guardian, Sir William Knollys (see Introduction, page 30). But there must have been quite a number of Malls whose pictures took dust – that is, who lost their good name – around 1600. If the allusion is literary, it could be to the sub-plot of Marston's *Jack Drum's Entertainment* (1600), a play which has some interesting verbal parallels with *Twelfth Night.*

122 *coranto* (a fast, skipping dance)

123 *sink-apace.* The French '*cinquepas*', or five-step dance, was very similar to the galliard. There is a quibble on 'sink' meaning 'sewer'. Beatrice quibbles differently with the word in *Much Ado About Nothing*, II.1.66–71.

126 *the star of a galliard* a dancing star (another recollection of Beatrice)

128 *dun-coloured stock* brown-coloured stocking. From what is known of Elizabethan handwriting, this is the most convincing of many emendations suggested for the Folio's *dam'd colour'd.*

130 *Taurus.* The twelve constellations, of which Taurus, the Bull, is one, were each held to govern a different part of the body.

I.4.2 *Cesario.* Viola's assumed name could come from Curio Gonzaga's comedy, *Gl'Inganni*, published in 1592, in which the heroine disguises as a page and assumes the name of Cesare. This has been taken as evidence that when Manningham said *Twelfth Night* resembled *Gl'Inganni* he meant Gonzaga's play, and not *Gl'Ingannati*. But there are very few other resemblances between Shakespeare's play and Gonzaga's. In the Italian and French tales based on *Gl'Ingannati* which Shakespeare certainly did read, the heroine calls herself Romulo or Romule because she is from Rome, and in making Viola call herself Cesario, which has the same associations, Shakespeare may be echoing these narrative versions.

5 *his humour* the changefulness of his disposition

6–7 *Is he inconstant . . .?* (asked with anxiety)

15 *address thy gait* direct your steps

16 *access*. This is accented on the second syllable.

28 *nuncio* messenger

aspect. This is accented on the second syllable.

32 *rubious* ruby-red

pipe voice

33 *sound* unbroken

34 *semblative* like, resembling

part (a theatrical term; Shakespeare is thinking of his company's boy actors)

35 *constellation* character (as decided by the stars)

39–40 *And thou shalt live as freely as thy lord . . . thine*. Orsino speaks more truly than he knows.

41 *barful strife* struggle to overcome my disinclination (to woo on Orsino's behalf)

I.5 (stage direction) *Feste*. 'Clown' in all speech-headings of the 1623 text. The name suggests a feast or festivity.

3 *hang thee* (an exaggeration, like 'You'll be shot')

5 *fear no colours*. In using this catchphrase for 'fear nothing' Feste puns on 'colours' and 'collars'. Maria in her reply reverts to the original meaning of 'colours' in this phrase – 'military standards'.

6 *Make that good* explain that

8 *good lenten answer* thin joke

13–14 *Well, God give them wisdom that have it . . . talents*. Feste's special line in jesting is a mock sanctimoniousness, which often gives his speech a biblical flavour. Here there are echoes of 'To him that hath shall be given' and of the parable of the good steward who put out his talent to usury. Feste implies that his seeming foolishness is a God-given insight.

16 *turned away* dismissed

19 *let summer bear it out* may the fine weather hold! In the same way the dismissed Fool in *Two Maids of More-*

clacke (printed 1608, acted earlier), a part played by Armin, says 'the summer's day is long, the winter's nights be short'.

21 *points*. Maria seizes on the meaning 'laces to hold up breeches', perhaps with a pun on *resolvo* (Latin), 'untie'.

23 *gaskins* loose breeches

25–6 *if Sir Toby ... Illyria*. This gives a hint of the marriage which is to occur before the end of the play.

28 *you were best* it would be best for you

(stage direction) *Malvolio*. It is just, but only just, conceivable that this name was suggested to Shakespeare by the name of Messer Agnol Malevolti, a lovesick character in the Italian play *Il Sacrificio*, which was acted as a form of curtain-raiser to *Gl'Ingannati*. It is if anything a little less conceivable that the name means 'I-want-Mall' and refers to Sir William Knollys's infatuation with Mary Fitton (see Introduction, page 30, and note on I.3.120). Shakespeare could have made up this name, suggestive of churlishness and misplaced desire, himself – influenced maybe by the expression '*mala volgia*' which occurs several times in Bandello's Italian version of the tale. But compare 'Benvolio' in *Romeo and Juliet*.

29 *Wit* intelligence

32 *Quinapalus*. Feste takes off the pedantry of quoting obscure authorities. This no longer gets a laugh, and the actor may be grateful for Leslie Hotson's suggestion that Feste here pretends to consult the carved head on his fool's stick, or bauble – even if he cannot accept the explanation that '*quinapalo*' is an italianate nonce-word for 'there on a stick'.

36 *Go to* (an expression of impatience, like our 'Come, come')

dry barren (of jests)

37 *dishonest* unreliable

40–42 *mend*. Feste plays with the meanings 'repair' and 'reform'.

42 *botcher* tailor who does repairs

45 *simple syllogism.* In this quibbling parody of formal deductive reasoning, Feste reminds Olivia that she must not expect too much of her fool, who is a mixture of vices and virtues like the rest of humanity; he then moves easily on to the suggestion that she should not expect her own grief to be unnaturally prolonged.

46 *no true cuckold but calamity.* Olivia seems, like Juliet, to be 'wedded to calamity'; but no one can mourn for ever – nor should Olivia try to do so, since while she tries her beauty will fade. There is probably a pun on *cuckold* and 'cockle' meaning 'weed'.

50 *Misprision* wrongful arrest (with a play on the more common meaning of 'misunderstanding')

50–51 *cucullus non facit monachum* the cowl does not make the monk (Latin proverb)

55 *Dexteriously* (a common Elizabethan variant of 'dexterously')

57–8 *Good my mouse of virtue.* Assuming his Sir Topas voice, Feste speaks to Olivia as a priest catechizing a small girl.

59 *idleness* pastime
bide abide, wait for

69 *mend* improve

71–2 *Infirmity, that decays the wise, doth ever make the better fool.* The bitterness of Malvolio's reply is due to his realization that Olivia has forgiven Feste, and is not going to turn him away.

75 *no fox* not cunning. By emphasizing 'I', Feste shows he is aware of Malvolio's scheming.

79 *put down* defeated in repartee

80 *ordinary fool . . . stone.* If this is a reference to Stone the Fool, a well-known Elizabethan jester, *ordinary* means 'of a tavern or eating-house'. Stone is called a tavern fool in Ben Jonson's *Volpone*, II.1.53–4.

81 *he's out of his guard* he has used up all his retorts (a fencing metaphor)

82 *minister occasion* supply opportunity

83 *set* (not spontaneous)

84 *zanies.* These were the professional fools' 'stooges' who fed them with matter for jests and unsuccessfully imitated their tricks. Olivia naturally resents this description of her father and herself.

87 *free* magnanimous. Like 'generous', the word suggests good breeding.

87–8 *bird-bolts* short, blunt arrows

89 *allowed* licensed

90 *known discreet man.* Olivia, regaining her equanimity, tactfully turns her reproach into a compliment.

92 *Mercury endue thee with leasing* may the god of deception make you a good liar

98 *well attended* with several attendants

108 *Jove.* Here and elsewhere this is almost certainly a substitution for 'God' in the play's original text, and must have been made after 27 May 1606, when a statute was passed against stage profanity.

110 *pia mater* brain (actually the membrane covering the brain)

115 *here.* The Folio 'heere' may represent a stage direction which indicated a hiccup.

116 *sot* fool

123 *an* if

124 *faith.* Strengthened more by faith than works, Sir Toby lurches out to defy the devil.
(stage direction) *followed by Maria.* Maria's exit is not marked in the Folio. The producer may prefer to make her leave later with Feste.

127 *above heat* above a normal temperature. Drink was thought to heat the blood.

129 *crowner* coroner

143 *sheriff's post.* A post was set up to mark the house of the civic authority. The custom persists in Scotland.

146 *of mankind* fierce. Leontes calls Paulina 'A mankind witch' in *The Winter's Tale*, II.3.67.

148–9 *will you or no* whether or not you are willing

150 *personage* appearance

152 *a squash* an unripe peascod

153 *a codling* an unripe apple

153–4 *in standing water* at the turn of the tide

154–5 *well-favoured* handsome

155 *shrewishly* sharply and like a woman

167 *con* learn by heart

168–9 *comptible, even to the least sinister usage* sensitive to even the least slight

173 *modest assurance* just enough assurance to satisfy me

175 *a comedian* an actor

176–7 *my profound heart . . . fangs of malice.* Viola acknowledges Olivia's penetration, but protests at her maliciousness.

179 *usurp* counterfeit. Viola takes the word in a more literal sense, as meaning 'to exercise a power which is not yours by right'.

182 *from my commission* not part of my instructions

185 *forgive* excuse (from delivering)

188 *feigned.* This may be an echo of *As You Like It*, where Touchstone maintains (III.3.17–18) that 'the truest poetry is the most feigning'.

190–91 *If you be not mad . . . if you have reason.* The antithesis here is between partial sanity and complete sanity, or reason. There is no need to emend.

192 *'Tis not that time of moon with me* I am not sufficiently lunatic

196 *swabber* deckhand. Viola retorts in Maria's own nautical language.

hull drift with furled sails

197 *Some mollification for* pray pacify

giant (used ironically of Maria)

197–8 *Tell me your mind.* Nearly all editors give this to Olivia. But Viola thinks she is on the point of being dismissed, and wants at least to be able to take back a message to Orsino. Olivia, however, is becoming increasingly interested in Viola, and asks her to deliver whatever message she has been entrusted with. This emboldens

Viola to ask that all bystanders should be sent out of earshot.

200 *courtesy* preliminary greetings (said ironically, either of Viola's behaviour at the gate or of a scuffle at the door with Maria)

fearful alarming

Speak your office tell me what you have been entrusted with

201 *It alone concerns your ear* it is meant to be heard only by you

202 *taxation of homage* demand for money to be paid as an acknowledgement of vassalage

207 *entertainment* reception

208–9 *divinity . . . profanation* (the language of the religion of love)

213 *comfortable* comforting

217 *by the method* in the same style

222 *are now out of your text* have changed the subject

224 *such a one I was this present* this is a recent portrait of me. Olivia throws back her veil as if she were revealing a curtained picture of herself.

227 *'Tis in grain* the colour is fast

228 *blent* blended. Viola keeps up the image of a painting.

229 *cunning* skilful

232 *copy*. Viola means a child, but Olivia pounces on the literal meaning.

234 *divers schedules* various lists

235 *labelled* attached as a codicil

236 *indifferent* fairly

238 *praise* appraise, estimate

243 *The nonpareil of beauty* the one unmatched in beauty

244 *fertile* copious

249 *In voices well divulged* well spoken of

free well bred. Orsino has the courtier's, scholar's, and soldier's qualities, and so represents, like Hamlet, the Renaissance ideal.

251 *A gracious person* endowed with a good physique

257 *willow* (associated with rejected love, as in the willow song in *Othello*)

258 *my soul* (Olivia)

259 *cantons* songs (from Italian '*canzone*', by confusion with 'canto' from Latin '*cantus*')

261 *Hallow*. The Folio spelling for 'halloo' is kept, because it conveys also the idea of 'bless'.

262 *babbling gossip* (Echo personified)

265 *But* unless

267 *state* social standing

273 *fee'd post* messenger to be tipped

275 *Love make* may the god of love make
that you shall love (the man) whom you will love

282 *blazon* a coat of arms. Cesario's bearing declares his high birth.

285 *perfections* (pronounced as four syllables)

291 *County*. This was a common Elizabethan form of 'count', keeping the two syllables of the Old French '*contē*'.

292 *Would I or not* whether I wanted it or not

293 *flatter with* encourage

299 *Mine eye too great a flatterer for my mind* my eye will betray my reason into thinking too well of him (Cesario)

300 *owe* own, control

II.1–2 *will you not that I go* do you not want me to go

3 *By your patience* if you will be so forbearing

4 *malignancy* evil influence (an astrological term)

5 *distemper* disorder, disturb

9 *sooth* indeed

9–10 *my determinate voyage is mere extravagancy* I only intend to wander

12–13 *it charges me in manners the rather to express myself* courtesy obliges me all the more to reveal who I am

15 *Messaline*. This is probably the modern Marseilles. The inhabitants of Marseilles and of Illyria are mentioned together ('*Massiliensis, Hilurios*') in a speech about one

twin looking for another twin in Plautus's *Menaechmi*, line 235. Shakespeare could also have had the word suggested to him by the occurrence of Messilina as a name in the story preceding 'Apolonius and Silla' in Rich's *Farewell to Military Profession*.

17 *in an hour* at the same time

20 *breach* surf, breakers

24 *estimable* appreciative. Sebastian means that he could not, in modesty, go so far as to marvel at the beauty of his twin sister.

25 *publish* speak openly of

28 *with more* with more salt water (that is, with tears)

29 *entertainment* treatment as my guest

31 *murder me for my love* cause me to die of grief at leaving you. Sebastian's reply is just as exaggerated: he would rather die than let Antonio demean himself by waiting on him.

34 *desire* request

35 *kindness* tender feelings

37 *tell tales of me* betray my feelings (by tears)

II.2 (stage direction) *several doors* separate entrances. The doors are those leading on to the stage or acting area; the scene itself is unlocalized.

1 *even* just

4 *arrived but hither* come only this far

8 *desperate assurance* certainty beyond all hope

she will none of him she wants nothing to do with him

12 *She took the ring of me* (a quick-witted lie to conceal Olivia's indiscretion from her steward)

of from

15 *in your eye* where you can see it

18 *charmed* cast a spell over

19 *made good view of me* examined me closely

20 *lost* lost touch with, failed to coordinate with

22 *cunning* craftiness

28 *the pregnant enemy* (Satan)
pregnant wily

29 *proper false* handsome deceivers

30–31 *Alas, our frailty is the cause, not we, | For such as we are made, if such we be.* These lines continue the idea of something being formed or made, like a wax seal: 'Alas, women's frailty is the cause, not women themselves, for what happens to us – if we are like that.' The lines make reasonable sense, but are not easy to get across in a theatre, and producers may prefer the emendation accepted by many editors: *Alas, our frailty is the cause, not we! | For such as we are made of, such we be.*

33 *fadge* turn out

34 *monster* (neither man nor woman)
fond dote

39 *thriftless* wasted, useless

II.3.2 *betimes* early
diluculo surgere. The adage '*dīlūculo sūrgere salūberrimum est*' ('to get up at dawn is most healthy') occurs in Lilly's Latin Grammar, a popular sixteenth-century schoolbook.

4 *troth* faith

9 *four elements* (the basic components of the world – fire, air, water, earth)

13 *stoup* (pronounced 'stoop') two-pint jug

16 *We Three.* Trick pictures, or anamorphoses, with this title were common at the time. One such picture shows a fool's head if viewed the right way up and another fool's head if viewed upside down. The spectator who asked 'Where's the third?' would be invited to view the picture from the side, where it took on the form of a donkey, and would then be asked (in Bottom's words) 'You see an ass head of your own, do you?' Hence Sir Toby's retort of 'Welcome, ass!'

17 *catch* round (a song with a continuous melody that could

be divided into parts, each harmonizing with the others)

18 *breast* singing voice

19 *leg* (the bow with which Feste begins and ends his songs)

21 *gracious* talented, inspired

22 *Pigrogromitus, of the Vapians passing the equinoctial of Queubus.* Feste's astronomical patter is mock-learning of the kind he later displays as Sir Topas. The names are probably Shakespeare's invention.

24 *leman* sweetheart

25 *impetticoat* (for Folio 'impeticos') pocket (in reference to the fool's long coat; a nonce-word)

gratillity little tip (another nonce-word, probably a diminutive formed from 'gratuity')

25–7 *Malvolio's nose is no whipstock, my lady has a white hand, and the Myrmidons are no bottle-ale houses.* No explanation satisfactorily connects these three statements. If *whipstock* means a wooden post or handle, Feste is saying Malvolio's nose is sensitive enough to smell out Sir Andrew's tip. If it means 'the piece of wood attached to a ship's tiller', he is saying much the same thing – that Malvolio can't be led by the nose. One attractive suggestion is that Malvolio, by reason of his haughty hooked nose (not straight like a whipstock), seems destined for greatness, and Olivia is ripe for marriage, a meaning of 'white hand' found in several Shakespeare plays; but the conclusion, that Malvolio is an upstart who as a Count will abolish cakes and ale, is less convincing. *My lady* could be Feste's leman, who likes to be taken to the most expensive inns such as the Myrmidons (perhaps with a pun on 'Mermaidens').

32 *testril* sixpence (a variant of 'tester')

33 *give a –.* As there is no point here in an interruption, it appears that a line was passed over by the compositor.

34 *a song of good life* a drinking song. But Sir Andrew takes it to be a moral song or hymn.

37 *O mistress mine!* Two instrumental versions of a tune with this title are known: one for a small band, by Thomas Morley, was published in 1599 and the other,

for keyboard, by William Byrd, was published in 1619. A modern transcription of Morley's air is given on page 194. Both pieces may be based on a popular Elizabethan tune to which Armin also sang Shakespeare's lyric. But we cannot be sure that Shakespeare intended to use this tune, which also occurs in an early seventeenth-century commonplace book as the setting for a quite different lyric.

40 *sweeting* darling

42 *Every wise man's son* (in allusion to the saying that wise men have fools for their sons)

52 *contagious.* Sir Toby means 'catchy', but Sir Andrew's 'sweet and contagious' sounds so odd, in view of the usual meaning of 'contagious' – 'infectious, evil-smelling' – that Sir Toby goes on to echo Sir Andrew ('dulcet in contagion') and say that a phrase like this could be used only if we heard with our noses. Shakespeare may have remembered an equally forced use of 'contagious' in 'Apolonius and Silla': 'But Silla, the further that she saw herself bereaved of all hope ever any more to see her beloved Apolonius, so much the more contagious were her passions ...' (*Elizabethan Love Stories*, ed. T. J. B. Spencer, p. 100; see Further Reading).

55 *welkin* sky

56–7 *three souls out of one weaver.* Sir Toby boasts that their catch will not only make the sky dance, but will have three times the usual effect of music on a pious weaver. Weavers were often Calvinist refugees from the Low Countries, who would be in ecstasy on hearing a well-sung psalm; and someone in an ecstasy appears to be without movement, feeling, or thought, and so without the three souls – of motion, feeling, and sense – which man was held to possess by the medieval philosophers.

58 *An* if

dog at clever at

63 *Hold thy peace.* A tune for this round is given on page

195. The effect when it is sung is that of a brawl, with each singer calling the others 'knave'.

73 *Cataian* Chinese. Olivia is inscrutable.
politicians schemers

74 *Peg-a-Ramsey.* A ballad about a jealous, spying wife was sung to this popular Elizabethan dance tune, so Sir Toby, if he is not so drunk that he is talking nonsense, may mean that Malvolio is keeping a watchful eye on the 'politicians'.

75 *Three merry men.* We have the words, but not the music, of several Elizabethan songs ending with this phrase. The music given on page 196 is that of a round in a collection made by the early seventeenth-century composer William Lawes, of which the final line was originally 'And three merry boys, and three merry boys, and three merry boys are we.'

77 *Tilly-vally!* It has been suggested that this is another snatch of song, as a tune has been found with the title 'Tilly-vally, any money'. But it is more probably an exclamation of impatience on Sir Toby's part.

78 *There dwelt a man in Babylon.* In mocking Maria's use of 'lady', Sir Toby recalls a ballad about Susanna and the Elders which has this word for its refrain. The first stanza is quoted in Percy's *Reliques of Ancient English Poetry*, ii. x:

> There dwelt a man in Babylon
> Of reputation great by fame;
> He took to wife a fair woman,
> Susanna she was called by name:
> A woman fair and virtuous;
> Lady, lady:
> Why should we not of her learn thus
> To live godly?

79 *Beshrew me* curse me

81–2 *grace . . . natural.* By making use of the theological distinction between grace and nature, Sir Andrew inadvertently calls himself a 'natural' fool.

83 *O' the twelfth day of December.* No song beginning with these words is known. Sir Toby may be misquoting the ballad of 'Musselburgh Field', which starts 'On the tenth day of December'. Or his words could be a misquotation of the first line of the carol called 'The Twelve Days of Christmas', which traditionally begins 'On the twelfth day . . .' and not as it is usually sung nowadays 'On the first day . . .'.

86 *wit* sense

honesty decency

87 *tinkers.* These were noted for their songs and their drinking. In *Egregious Popish Impostures* (1603), Richard Harsnet writes about a 'master setter of catches or rounds, used to be sung by tinkers as they sit by the fire with a pot of good ale between their legs'.

89 *coziers* cobblers (who also sang at their work)

89–90 *mitigation or remorse of voice* lowering your voices out of consideration

92 *Sneck up!* buzz off! Originally meaning 'Go and be hanged', this survives in both American and British dialects with the meaning 'Make yourself scarce!'

93 *round* blunt

99 *Farewell, dear heart.* Sir Toby and Feste sing their own version of a song which is given in Robert Jones's *First Book of Airs*, 1600. See page 198.

104 *there you lie.* Probably Sir Toby has fallen over.

110 *Out o'tune* (a way of refuting Feste's denial and taking his 'dare')

112 *cakes and ale.* These were traditional at Church feasts, and so repugnant to Puritans, who would also be offended at the mention of Saint Anne, mother of the Virgin Mary.

113 *ginger.* This was a favourite Elizabethan spice, and the sheep-shearing feast in *The Winter's Tale* calls for a root or two of ginger. Robert Armin liked ginger washed down with ale.

116 *chain* chain of office. There is a reference to this method

of cleaning such insignia in Webster's *The Duchess of Malfi*, III.2. Sir Toby is reminding Malvolio of his station in Olivia's household.

121 *shake your ears* (a contemptuous dismissal, equivalent to calling Malvolio a donkey)

123 *challenge him the field* challenge him to a duel. The suggestion shows Sir Andrew's ill breeding, as it was a social solecism to challenge an inferior.

130 *gull* trick

nayword byword

131 *common recreation* source of amusement for everyone

133 *Possess us* give us the facts

136 *exquisite* (a difficult word for the drunken knights to get their tongues round. Shakespeare puts it twice in the mouth of Cassio, to mark his increasing drunkenness, in *Othello*, II.3.18, 93)

141 *time-pleaser* time-server

affectioned affected

141–2 *cons state without book* learns high-sounding phrases by heart

142 *swathes.* A swathe is the grass cut at a single sweep of a scythe. The image is of a huge circuitous period falling like hay about the listener's ears.

142–3 *the best persuaded of himself* thinking better of himself than anyone else does

150 *expressure* expression

152 *feelingly personated* vividly described

163 *Ass* (Maria puns on 'as' and 'ass')

165 *physic* medicine (to purge Malvolio's conceit)

166–7 *let the fool make a third.* See Introduction, page 20, on Shakespeare's probable change of plan here. It is odd that Feste himself says nothing in this part of the scene. Producers have sometimes made him exit in the wake of Malvolio, or even fall asleep until the end of the scene.

168 *construction* interpretation

170 *Penthesilea* (an Amazonian queen. Maria's spirit is out of all proportion to her size.)

172 *beagle* (a small but keen and intelligent hound)

177 *recover* get hold of

178 *out* out of pocket

180 *cut* (a term of contempt, in reference to a cut horse, or gelding)

183 *burn some sack* warm and spice some Spanish wine

II.4.1 *good morrow* good morning

2 *good Cesario*. It has been suggested that Shakespeare altered this scene to make Feste the singer, and that this opening indicates his original intention of having Viola sing the song. But Orsino may simply be inviting Viola to listen to the song with him. See Introduction, pages 18–19.

3 *antique* strange and old-world

5 *recollected terms* studied phrases. New-fangled words accompanied new-fangled music: 'airs' were all the rage around 1601.

18 *Unstaid* unsteady

motions emotions

21–2 *It gives a very echo to the seat | Where love is throned* it awakens an immediate response in the heart

22 *masterly* from experience, as one who has mastered the art of love

24 *favour* face

25 *by your favour*. A slight stress on *your* shows that Viola is playing with the meanings 'if you please' and 'like you in feature'.

29 *still* always

30 *wears she* she adapts herself

31 *sways she level in her husband's heart* her husband's love for her remains steady

34 *worn* exhausted. Orsino seems inconstant even to his belief in his own constancy.

35 *I think it well*. Viola says this hesitantly and with mixed feelings, since she both wants and does not want Orsino

to be inconstant. The plot unties this particular knot for her.

37 *hold the bent* remain at full stretch (a metaphor from archery)

39 *displayed* unfolded, open (not merely 'shown')

44 *spinsters* spinners

45 *free*. This can mean either 'unattached' or 'free from care'. To Orsino these are one and the same thing.

weave their thread with bones make lace on bone bobbins

46 *silly sooth* simple truth

47 *dallies with* dwells on

48 *the old age* the good old days

50 *Come away, come away, death*. No contemporary setting of this has been discovered.

51 *cypress*. This could be either a coffin of cypress wood or a bier decorated with boughs of cypress. There are references to both in the period.

52 *Fie away!* be off!

56 *My part of death, no one so true | Did share it* no one so faithful has ever received his allotted portion, death

60 *greet* bewail. This verb was no longer used transitively in the sixteenth century, but perhaps this is one of the things that give Feste's song its antique flavour.

67 *No pains, sir*. Feste seems to resent Orsino's offhand payment.

69 *pleasure will be paid* (proverbial)

71 *leave, to leave thee* (a courteous dismissal)

72 *the melancholy god* (Saturn, whose planet ruled those of a melancholy humour)

73 *changeable* shot (having the weft of one colour and the woof of another so that the material shows different colours when viewed from different angles)

74 *opal* (semi-precious stone which changes colour with changes in the light)

74–7 *I would . . . nothing*. The captain of a merchant ship with no fixed schedule would be able to pick up cargoes easily.

80 *the world* society

82 *parts* gifts of wealth and position

83 *giddily* lightly, carelessly. Fortune was a fickle goddess.

84 *that miracle* (her beauty)

85 *pranks* adorns

87 *Sooth* in truth

93 *bide* bear

95–8 *retention . . . cloyment, and revolt.* 'Retention' is a medical term meaning 'the power to retain'. Orsino is not speaking metaphorically; in Shakespeare's day, the emotions were held to have physiological origins. Thus the liver (generative of the digestive juices) is not only to the appetite as real passion is to a passing fancy, but is itself the seat of the passions. See also I.1.38–9.

111 *damask.* The contrast with 'green and yellow melancholy', suggesting the unhealthy pallor of grief, shows that the mingled pink and white of the damask rose is meant here.

113 *Patience on a monument.* Both here and in *Pericles* V.1.137–8 – 'Like Patience gazing on kings' graves, and smiling | Extremity out of act' – Shakespeare has in mind some such allegorical figure as the representation of Patience in *Iconologia* (1593), a popular Elizabethan reference book, where she is seated on a stone with a yoke on her shoulders and her feet on thorns.

116 *Our shows are more than will* we display more passion than we actually feel

120 *And all the brothers too.* Viola remembers Sebastian with these words, and the thought deepens the scene's melancholy.

123 *denay* denial

II.5 (stage direction) *Fabian.* This name may echo 'Fabio', the girl-page's assumed name in *Gl'Ingannati.* On Feste's replacement by Fabian, see Introduction, page 20. Fabian's position in Olivia's household seems to be that of a 'hanger-on', rather than of a paid servant.

3 *boiled to death* (a piece of facetiousness; melancholy was a cold humour)

5 *sheep-biter* (originally a dog that attacks sheep; so a slang word meaning a sneaking fellow)

8 *bear-baiting*. This explanation of Fabian's presence fits in with the mention of Malvolio as a kind of Puritan; the Puritans were fiercely opposed to bear-baiting.

12 *An* if

14 *metal of India* pure gold (with a pun on 'mettle')

19 *a contemplative idiot* the kind of imbecile who gazes into vacuity

Close hide

22 *tickling* flattery. Trout can be caught in shallow pools by rubbing them round the gills.

24 *affect* care for

26 *complexion* temperament

31 *jets* struts

32 *'Slight* (an oath – 'by God's light')

38–9 *The lady of the Strachy married the yeoman of the wardrobe*. One recent explanation of this is that William Strachy was a shareholder in the Children's company at Blackfriars Theatre early in the seventeenth century, and either he or his wife visited the theatre two or three times a week to collect their share of the takings in the presence of David Yeomans, tiresman (wardrobe-keeper) of the company, whom Strachy's widow can be presumed eventually to have married. But if the allusion is in fact to these people, it must have been added to the play a very little time before it was printed in the Folio, as William Strachy did not die till 1621. The two definite articles make it hard to accept this statement as an allusion to Strachy's wife and David Yeomans. 'Yeoman of a wardrobe' was a generic name for a tiresman, but *the* Wardrobe usually meant the Queen's Wardrobe in the Blackfriars precinct – as it does in Shakespeare's will. *The* Strachy sounds like the name of a house rather than a man. Probably the allusion is to a piece of

Blackfriars or Court gossip of 1601 or 1602 which is not recorded elsewhere.

40 *Jezebel* (the shameless wife of King Ahab; see I Kings 16. 31 onwards)

42 *blows him* puffs him up

44 *state* canopied chair of state

45 *stone-bow* (cross-bow from which small stones could be shot)

46–7 *branched velvet* velvet brocade

51 *to have the humour of state* to be up on my dignity

52 *demure travel of regard* grave look round the company

58 *make out* go out

59 *with my –.* Malvolio is fingering his steward's chain of office when he suddenly realizes he will no longer be wearing it.

61 *curtsies* bows low

63–4 *Though our silence be drawn from us with cars, yet peace!* This resembles the modern 'Wild horses wouldn't draw it out of me.' Fabian is saying 'Keep quiet, though it is a torment to do so.'

cars chariots

74 *scab* scurvy fellow

81 *employment* business, matter

83 *woodcock* (an easily trapped bird)

gin snare

84–5 *the spirit of humours intimate reading aloud to him* may he take it into his head to read aloud

spirit of humours genius who guides the capricious

86–8 *These be her . . . great P's.* Not all these letters occur in the superscription, but they are given to Malvolio to make him sound bawdy. 'Cut' is the female organ.

87–8 *makes . . . P's* (with a play on the meaning 'urinates')

88 *in contempt of question* beyond all doubt

91 *Soft!* gently! (as he breaks the seal)

92 *impressure* stamp, seal

Lucrece (seal bearing the image of the Roman matron Lucretia, the model of chastity)

94 *liver and all*. Malvolio is deeply excited.

99–100 *The numbers altered!* the metre is changed!

102 *brock* badger. Malvolio is burrowing for the letter's meaning.

106 *M.O.A.I.* Shakespeare scholars have been no quicker than Malvolio at solving this fustian riddle. An attractive suggestion is that the letters stand for I AM O (I am Olivia and this rules my conduct), but that Malvolio, sick of self-love, immediately applies them to himself, thus provoking Sir Toby's remark about a cold scent.

107 *fustian* wretched

112 *staniel* (an inferior hawk)

checks at it swerves to pounce on it (a hawking term)

115 *formal capacity* normal intelligence

115–16 *obstruction* difficulty

117 *position* arrangement

120–21 *Sowter will cry . . . rank as a fox*. Malvolio has missed the right meaning and is about to go full cry after his own interpretation, like a hound which has missed the hare's scent and picked up a fox's instead. *Sowter* means 'cobbler' and is presumably a name for an awkward hound.

125 *faults* breaks in the scent

126 *consonancy* consistency

127 *that suffers under probation* that will stand up to investigation

129 *O shall end*. 'O' could mean the hangman's noose. But if the riddle means 'I AM O', Fabian may be hoping that Malvolio will work it out.

135 *simulation* disguise

135–6 *the former* (referring to 'I may command where I adore')

139 *revolve* consider

140 *born*. The Folio has 'become'. The sentence is repeated twice later in the play, with *born* in each case, so we must assume the compositor read 'borne' as 'become' – a plausible error. Maria's letter is not italicized in the

Folio after *revolve*, which suggests that only the beginning of it was in the promptbook, and that this had to be supplemented by the letter read out on the stage. This is also suggested by the end of the letter, where the Folio reads 'tht fortunate vnhappy daylight and champian' with an awkward space after 'vnhappy'. The punctuation of the letter is also uncertain, by comparison with the careful punctuation of the rest of the play. A property letter would be less legible than the promptbook, either because of rough handling or because it was a piece of the author's manuscript, and this might explain 'become' as a misreading of 'borne'.

144 *slough* (a snake's old skin)

145 *opposite with* hostile towards

146 *tang* resound

146–7 *trick of singularity* affectation of oddness

148 *yellow stockings*. Not only were these old-fashioned by 1602, but they would be out of keeping with the deep mourning of Olivia's household. It is hard to believe that Olivia ever 'commended' them, if she abhorred the colour yellow (line 192 below). Probably the only commendation is in this letter, and Shakespeare shows us how Malvolio's imagination does the rest.

149 *cross-gartered* wearing garters which crossed at the back of the knee and tied above it in front. This custom was old-fashioned at the date of the play.

154 *Daylight and champain discovers not more* broad daylight and open country couldn't make this more plain

156 *baffle* disgrace (used of a knight)

157 *point-devise* to the last detail

158 *jade* deceive

163 *habits* clothes

164 *strange* aloof

stout bold

169 *dear*. Possibly the Folio 'deero' is not a misprint for 'deere', and we should read 'dear, O my sweet'.

174 *Sophy* Shah of Persia. This may be an allusion to the

gifts heaped on Sir Anthony Shirley by the Shah. See Introduction, page 21.

180 *gull-catcher* one who traps fools

183 *tray-trip* (a dicing game in which success depends on throwing a three)

189 *aqua-vitae* spirits

196 *a notable contempt* an infamous disgrace

198 *Tartar* Tartarus (the classical name for hell)

III.1 (stage direction) *tabor*. Queen Elizabeth's jester Tarlton is shown in a famous engraving playing a tabor, or small drum, and a pipe. The only real break in the play's action occurs between Acts II and III, and perhaps Feste has been entertaining the audience in this interval by playing his pipe and tabor.

1 *Save thee* God save thee

live by make a living by

8 *lies by* dwells near (playing on the meaning 'go to bed with')

9 *stands by* (with a play on the meaning 'is upheld by')

12 *cheveril* kid leather

14 *dally nicely* play subtly

15 *wanton* equivocal. Feste goes on to play with the meaning 'unchaste'.

19–20 *words are very rascals, since bonds disgraced them.* This is often read as an allusion to the Jesuit practice of equivocation. But Feste can simply be moralizing by saying that frequent demands for vows and pledges show that a man's yea is no longer yea, nor his nay, nay.

22–4 *I can yield you . . . reason with them.* Feste, who is a wise fool, here touches on one of the biggest problems in philosophy.

33 *pilchers* pilchards (shoaling fish, similar to herrings)

40 *your wisdom* (an ironic courtesy title)

41 *an* if

pass upon jest at

43 *commodity* consignment

45 *By my troth* in faith

48 *these* (coins)

49 *use* interest

50 *Pandarus* (the go-between in the medieval story of Troilus and Cressida, on which Shakespeare wrote a tragedy. Feste hints that he will further a meeting between Olivia and Cesario if he is well tipped.)

53–4 *begging but a beggar* (in allusion to the practice of begging the guardianship of rich orphans from the sovereign)

54 *Cressida was a beggar.* She became one in Henryson's fifteenth-century poem, *The Testament of Cresseid.*

55 *conster* construe, explain

56 *out of my welkin* not my affair

56–7 *welkin . . . element.* In substituting a far-fetched word like *welkin*, which means 'sky', for *element*, Shakespeare may be defending Ben Jonson, whose use of the word 'element' had been satirized in a play by Dekker, *Satiromastix* (1601).

58–9 *This fellow is wise enough to play the fool . . . kind of wit.* This idea about the professional fool is a commonplace of the time, but it is possible that Shakespeare is remembering a set of verses in Robert Armin's *Quips upon Question* (1600):

> A merry man is often thought unwise;
> Yet mirth in modesty's loved of the wise.
> Then say, should he for a fool go,
> When he's a more fool that accounts him so?
> Many men descant on another's wit
> When they have less themselves in doing it.

62 *like the haggard, check at every feather* swoop on every small bird, as the wild hawk does. So Feste seizes every opportunity for a jest.

65 *fit* to the point

66 *folly-fallen, quite taint their wit* stooping to folly, considerably impair their reputation for common sense

69–70 *Dieu vous garde, monsieur! | Et vous aussi; votre serviteur!* God keep you, sir! And you too; your servant!

72 *encounter* approach. Sir Toby speaks affectedly, but Viola is a match for him.

73 *trade* business. Viola picks up the meaning 'a trading voyage'.

75 *list* objective

76 *Taste* try out

80 *gate and entrance*. This phrase has a legal flavour, and *gate* has a special legal meaning – 'the right to pasture'. There is a pun on 'gait'.

81 *prevented* forestalled

86 *pregnant* quick in understanding, receptive

vouchsafed attentive

88 *all ready*. Sir Andrew may write them down carefully.

95 *'Twas never merry world* (a catchphrase like the modern 'Things have never been the same')

96 *lowly feigning* pretended humility (in allusion to the mistress–servant convention of courtly love)

107 *music from the spheres*. In ancient astronomy, still widely accepted in Shakespeare's day, the universe was thought of as being constructed of crystalline spheres, so tightly fitted the one inside the other that they ground together as they turned and so produced music.

110 *abuse* impose upon

112 *hard construction* harsh interpretation

115 *at the stake* (an image from bear-baiting)

117 *receiving* perception

118 *cypress* piece of thin black gauze

121 *grize* flight of steps (which is also the literal meaning of *degree*, line 120)

vulgar proof common experience

124 *how apt the poor are to be proud*. Olivia refers to herself rather than to Viola – 'Though you reject me, I've

something to be proud of – I have fallen for a king among men.'

130 *proper* handsome

131 *due west*. Olivia is telling Cesario to go and seek his fortunes elsewhere.

westward ho! (the cry of the Thames watermen seeking passengers for the journey from the City to the Court at Westminster)

132 *good disposition* equanimity (a natural happiness, as distinct from that given by *grace*)

136 *That you do think you are not what you are*. Viola implies that Olivia is forgetting her worldly position.

137 *the same of you* (that you are not in fact what you are in appearance. Olivia suspects Cesario is a high-born youth in disguise.)

145 *love's night is noon* (love cannot be hid)

148 *I love thee so*. Olivia changes to the intimate second person singular.

maugre in spite of

149 *wit* common sense

150–53 *Do not extort thy reasons from this clause . . . is better* do not force yourself to think that because I have declared my love you ought not to love me, but rather restrain this way of thinking with the reflection that love which is freely given is better than love that has been begged

150 *clause* premise

151 *For that* because

III.2.10 *argument* proof

12 *'Slight!* by God's light!

13–14 *oaths of judgement and reason*. Theologians laid down three conditions for an oath: truth, judgement, reason. Fabian omits truth.

15 *grand-jury men*. The task of a grand jury was to decide if the evidence in particular cases was sufficient to

warrant a trial. Fabian goes on to produce evidence that Olivia is in love with Sir Andrew.

18 *dormouse* sleeping (but with a further implied meaning 'timid')

23 *baulked* shirked

23–4 *double gilt of this opportunity*. The most costly gold plate was twice gilded. We still speak of a golden opportunity.

25 *sailed into the north of my lady's opinion* earned my lady's cold disdain

26 *icicle on a Dutchman's beard*. This is probably an allusion to William Barentz's Arctic voyage in 1596–7.

28 *policy* diplomacy

30 *Brownist*. The Brownists were a religious group later called 'Independents' and (in the nineteenth century) 'Congregationalists'. Their advocacy of a very democratic form of Church government seemed highly seditious and 'political' to the average Elizabethan.

politician schemer

31–2 *build me ... Challenge me*. 'Me' here implies 'on my advice'.

40 *curst* petulant

42 *invention* inventiveness, matter

with the licence of ink with things you dare not say to his face

43 *'thou'-est* address him as 'thou' (that is, as an inferior)

45 *bed of Ware* (the famous Elizabethan bed, measuring over ten feet each way, now in the Victoria and Albert Museum in London)

46 *gall*. Sir Toby puns on the meanings 'an ingredient of ink' and 'bitterness'.

47 *goose* (symbolic of cowardice)

50 *cubiculo* bedroom (Italian – another affected term from Sir Toby)

51 *manikin* puppet

57 *wain-ropes* waggon-ropes pulled by oxen

58 *hale* drag

60 *anatomy* cadaver

63 *youngest wren of nine.* A wren lays nine or ten eggs and the last bird hatched is usually the smallest. This justifies the emendation from the Folio 'youngest Wren of mine', which has little meaning.

64 *the spleen* a fit of laughter

68 *impossible passages of grossness* wildly improbable statements (in Maria's letter)

71–2 *pedant that keeps a school i'the church* schoolmaster who, having no schoolhouse of his own, teaches in the church. The practice was oldfashioned by this period.

75–6 *the new map with the augmentation of the Indies.* Emmeric Mollineux's map of the world on a new projection, published in 1599, has a mesh of rhumb lines, and is the first to show the whole of the East Indies, which are therefore 'augmented'.

III.3.1 *troubled you* (to follow me to the city)

6 *not all* not only

8 *jealousy* concern

9 *skill-less in* unacquainted with

12 *rather* more speedily (the original meaning of the word)

16 *uncurrent* worthless (like coins out of currency)

17 *worth* means

conscience awareness of my debt to you

19 *reliques* antiquities, sights

24 *renown* make famous

27 *the Count his galleys* the Count's galleys

29 *it would scarce be answered* it would be difficult to make reparation

30 *Belike* perhaps

32–3 *Albeit the quality of the time and quarrel | Might well have given us bloody argument* although at that time, and with the cause we had, bloodshed could have been justified

35 *traffic's* trade's

37 *lapsèd* apprehended

40 *Elephant*. At the time this play was written, there was an inn called the Elephant in Southwark, near the Globe Theatre. The more famous Elephant and Castle, still in London's 'south suburbs', is not mentioned in documents until the middle of the seventeenth century.

41 *bespeak our diet* order our meals

45 *Haply* perhaps

toy trifle

47 *idle markets* unnecessary expenditure

III.4.1 *he says he'll come* supposing he says he'll come

2 *bestow of* give

5 *sad and civil* grave and sedate

9 *possessed* (by the devil)

22 *sonnet* song

'*Please one and please all*'. This is the refrain of a popular song of the time. Malvolio should perhaps squeak it out, to mark his transformation.

25–6 *Not black in my mind, though yellow in my legs* not melancholy (melancholy being caused by the black bile) in spite of the melancholy colour of my stockings. There is a possible allusion to a ballad tune called 'Black and Yellow', and perhaps Malvolio hums a little of it.

26 *It* (Maria's letter)

27 *sweet Roman hand* (fashionable new italic handwriting)

29–30 '*Ay, sweetheart, and I'll come to thee*'. This is a quotation from another popular song, of which the words are given in *Tarlton's Jests*, 1601.

35 *daws* jackdaws. The remark has more point if Malvolio has been singing.

47–8 *thy yellow stockings*. In quoting the letter, Malvolio appears to be calling his mistress 'thou' and she echoes him in shocked surprise at this familiarity.

56 *midsummer madness* (a proverbial phrase; great heat was supposed to make dogs run mad)

58 *hardly* only with difficulty

63 *miscarry* come to harm

65 *come near me* begin to understand who I am

71 *tang*. The Folio has 'langer'. The compositor had apparently no difficulty with the rather unusual word 'tang' in II.5.146, which suggests that the letter and this passage were in different handwritings, and that here the word ended with a flourish.

74 *the habit of some sir of note* the way of dressing of some very important personage (perhaps Sir William Knollys)

75 *limed* snared

76 *fellow*. This word originally meant 'companion', but was used to inferiors, with polite condescension, from the fourteenth century onwards. Malvolio flatters himself Olivia uses it of him as an equal.

79 *scruple*. Malvolio plays on the meanings 'doubt' and 'minute quantity'.

80 *incredulous* incredible

84 *in the name of sanctity*. Sir Toby invokes holy powers before his encounter with the possessed Malvolio.

85 *drawn in little* contracted to minute size (like Milton's devils in Pandaemonium)

Legion (used of the many devils possessing the madman described in Saint Mark 5.9)

89–90 *private* privacy

96 *Let me alone* let me deal with this

102 *wisewoman* herbalist

109 *move* upset

111 *rough* violent

112 *bawcock* fine bird

113 *chuck* chicken

115 *biddy* chickabiddy. Sir Toby is clucking encouragingly at Malvolio.

116 *gravity* a sober, mature man

cherry-pit (children's game played with cherry-stones)

117 *collier* coal-vendor (in allusion to the devil's blackness)

123 *element* sphere of existence

126 *played upon a stage*. This kind of theatrical bravado is found also in *Julius Caesar*, III.1.111–16, and *Antony and Cleopatra*, V.2.215–20. It does not imply that *Twelfth Night* was not originally acted on a stage.

128 *genius* soul

130–31 *take air, and taint* be exposed, and so spoilt. The Elizabethans thought fresh air bad for many fevers.

133 *quieter* freer from Malvolio's interference

134–5 *dark room and bound*. This was the usual treatment for insanity in the period. 'Love' (says Rosalind) 'is merely a madness and, I tell you, deserves as well a dark house and a whip as madmen do' (*As You Like It*, III.2.383–4).

139 *to the bar*. This is unexplained. It may mean the bar dividing the benchers from the students in hall in the Inns of Court.

139–40 *a finder of madmen* one of a jury appointed to find out if an accused person was insane

141 *matter for a May morning* sport fit for a holiday

144 *saucy* (with a pun on the meanings 'impudent' and 'piquant')

149 *admire* marvel

151–2 *keeps you from the blow of the law* shelters you from the law (that is, from being accused of causing a breach of the peace)

154 *thou liest in thy throat*. If Sir Andrew's letter is not as senseless as Fabian thinks, Sir Andrew is postulating a statement by Cesario: 'You are angry because of the Lady Olivia's attentions to me' in order to have grounds for calling him a liar.

161–2 *thou kill'st me like a rogue and a villain*. Sir Andrew's effort to avoid any actionable abuse, or any threat of violence towards his opponent, would have delighted an audience of law students.

163 *o' the windy side* on the safe side (because you can't be scented out)

166–7 *my hope* (of winning – but Sir Andrew is made to appear as if he is in hope of something better than salvation)

167–8 *as thou usest him* as thy usage of him deserves (not at all, in fact)

171 *commerce* conference

173 *Scout me for him* I want you to keep a look-out for him

174 *bum-baily* (bailiff, or sheriff's officer, who shadowed a debtor in order to arrest him)

178 *approbation* credit

proof trial, testing

186 *clodpole* blockhead

192 *cockatrices* (mythical monsters able to kill with a glance)

193 *Give them way* keep out of their way

194 *presently* immediately

195 *horrid* terrifying

198 *unchary* unguardedly

on't (on a heart of stone, in allusion to the Elizabethan custom of making payment of a debt on a known stone in a church)

202 *With the same 'haviour* in the same manner

204 *jewel* jewel-set miniature

208 *That honour saved may upon asking give* that honour may grant, when requested, without compromising itself

212–13 *Well, come again tomorrow. Fare thee well . . . bear my soul to hell.* The conclusive-sounding couplet here, and the fact that the action from this point to the end of the Act can be thought of as taking place in the street outside Olivia's garden, would justify a modern producer's treating the remainder of this Act as a separate scene. On the Elizabethan stage, however, the action is continuous. Sir Toby and Fabian come forward and intercept Viola outside the door (or the curtain concealing the back of the stage) by which Olivia has just left. Then Sir Toby crosses the stage and either goes out by the farthest door to bring Sir Andrew back at 'Why man, he's a very devil' (line 267), or, finding him in view of the audience, engages him in conversation and brings him downstage so that 'Why, man' are the first words heard by the audience. Sir Toby and Fabian then coax the duellists into coming face to face, and as soon as they do so Antonio makes his dramatic entry.

218 *despite* defiance

219–20 *Dismount thy tuck* draw thy sword

220 *yare* prompt

223 *remembrance* recollection

227 *opposite* opponent

228 *withal* with

230 *unhatched*. This means either 'not marked in battle' or 'never drawn'.

231 *on carpet consideration* for non-military services to the crown (usually financial ones at that period)

235 *Hob, nob* come what may (literally, have it or have it not)

239 *taste* test

quirk peculiarity

241 *computent* to be reckoned with

245 *meddle* engage in combat

248 *know of* inquire from

250 *purpose* intention

255 *mortal arbitrement* decision of the matter by mortal combat

259 *form* appearance

265 *Sir Priest*. *Sir* here stands for '*Dominus*', the title given to a graduate and thence used of a clergyman.

268 *firago* virago. The word means a fighting woman, but was used of both sexes in Shakespeare's day.

269 *stuck-in* thrust (from the Italian fencing term, '*stoccata*')

269–70 *mortal motion* deadly movement

270 *it is inevitable* it cannot be averted

270–71 *on the answer, he pays you* he counters your return blow

272 *to the Sophy*. Shakespeare may have learned from his former colleague Kemp, who had met Sir Anthony Shirley on his return from Persia, that Sir Robert Shirley had remained in the Shah's military service. See Introduction, page 21.

276 *An* if

280 *make the motion* put the proposal

281 *perdition of souls* (killing)

282 *Marry* (an asseveration – originally 'By Mary')

286 *He is as horribly conceited* he has as terrifying an idea

298 *duello* code of duelling

309 *an undertaker* one who undertakes another's quarrel

314 *that I promised* (the horse)

320 *favour* face

324 *answer* make reparation for

325–6 *What will you do, now my necessity | . . . purse?* Antonio's appeal, even in a desperate situation, expresses his concern for Sebastian.

328 *amazed* bewildered, dazed

329 *be of comfort* do not grieve

335 *having* resources

336 *my present* what I have at present

337 *coffer* money (literally, chest)

339–40 *Is't possible that my deserts to you | Can lack persuasion?* is it possible that the claims of my past kindnesses can fail to move you?

346 *vainness* boasting

352 *sanctity of love* love as for a sacred object

354 *venerable* worthy to be venerated

356 *vild* vile (a common Elizabethan form of the word, kept here for euphony)

358–9 *In nature, there's no blemish but the mind; | None can be called deformed, but the unkind* although there may seem to be deformities in nature, the only real deformity is a hard heart

361 *o'er-flourished* richly decorated. Elaborately carved or painted chests were a feature of prosperous Elizabethan homes.

365 *so do not I?* why do I not believe myself (my hope that my brother is alive)?

368 *Come hither*. Sir Toby and his friends draw contemptuously aside, leaving Viola to speak her thoughts in couplets, the common form for adages, or 'sage saws'.

369 *sage saws* wise sayings, aphorisms

370–71 *I my brother know* | *Yet living in my glass* I know my brother is the image of me

374 *prove* prove to be so

376 *dishonest* dishonourable

380 *religious in it* behaving as if it were a principle of his faith (to be cowardly)

381 *'Slid* (a mild oath – originally, 'God's eyelid')

385 *event* result

386 *yet* after all

IV.1.5 *held out* kept up

9 *vent* void, get rid of

13 *lubber* overgrown boy

14 *cockney* pampered child. Feste is saying 'How affected everyone is getting, using words like "vent"!'

ungird thy strangeness stop being stand-offish

15 *vent* utter, say. This meaning, developed from the meaning 'get rid of' (see line 9 above), was to become common in the seventeenth century.

17 *foolish Greek* buffoon. The expression is usually found in the form 'merry Greek'.

22 *after fourteen years' purchase*. The usual Elizabethan price of land was the equivalent of twelve years' rent, so *fourteen years' purchase* was a lot of money, and the phrase means 'at a price'.

33 *action of battery*. As Sir Andrew struck the first blow he has, of course, no case: another joke for the law students.

38 *put up your iron* sheathe your sword (said ironically; Sebastian has only used the hilt of his dagger)

fleshed initiated into fighting, blooded

43 *malapert* impudent

50 *Rudesby* boor

52 *uncivil* barbarous

extent assault (originally a legal term)

55 *botched up* crudely contrived

57 *deny* refuse

Beshrew curse

58 *started* roused (a hunting term)

heart (with a pun on 'hart' and a use of the familiar conceit that lovers exchange hearts)

59 *What relish is in this?* what am I to make of this?

relish taste

60 *Or* either

61 *Lethe* (the mythical river of forgetfulness)

63 *Would thou'dst* if only you would

IV.2.2 *Sir* (a title used for clergyman; see III.4.265, note)

Topas. All precious and semi-precious stones were supposed to have healing properties; the topaz cured lunacy.

curate parish priest

8 *said* called

an honest man and a good housekeeper a good sort, and hospitable

9 *careful* serious-minded

10 *competitors* confederates

12 *Bonos dies* good day (mock Latin)

12–13 *old hermit of Prague* (an authority invented in parody of pedantic name-dropping)

14 *Gorboduc* (legendary early British king, hero of a famous sixteenth-century play)

that that is, is. Feste takes off the axioms of medieval philosophy which often sound absurdly self-evident to the layman.

20 (stage direction) *within.* In the Folio, the stage direction *Maluolio within* precedes the speech-heading *Mal.*, as a warning to the actor to be ready. See An Account of the Text, page 185.

25 *hyperbolical* boisterous. Feste is addressing the devil which has possessed Malvolio.

33–4 *that house is dark.* A dark house was the term for a

darkened room in which a madman was confined. The expression occurs in the fifth story of Rich's *Farewell to Military Profession*.

36 *bay windows*. These were the rage of the period, when great houses were laughed at for being 'more glass than wall'.

36–7 *barricadoes* barricades. These and ebony wood are the most opaque things Feste can think of. His joke is of the 'clear as mud' type.

37 *clerestories* (a range of windows high up in a wall)

42 *darkness*. A three-day darkness was one of the plagues of Egypt described in Exodus 10.

47 *abused* ill treated

48 *constant question* question and answer on a normal topic

49 *Pythagoras* (a Greek philosopher who held the theory of the transmigration of souls; the same soul could inhabit in succession the bodies of different kinds of creatures – fish, birds, and animals, as well as men)

51 *haply* perhaps

62 *I am for all waters* I can turn my hand to anything (with a pun on 'water' in the sense of the brilliance or lustre of a precious or semi-precious stone such as a topaz)

63–4 *Thou . . . not*. This suggests an afterthought on Shakespeare's part, and so, rapid composition. See page 20.

69–70 *the upshot* to its final outcome (an archery term, meaning 'the decisive shot')

71 *Hey Robin, jolly Robin*. An early Tudor setting to this poem is given on page 200. The words have been attributed to Sir Thomas Wyatt.

74 *perdy* (an adjuration; French *par Dieu*)

86 *besides your five wits* out of your mind (the five wits being the five faculties of the mind: common wit, imagination, fantasy, estimation, and memory)

91 *propertied me* treated me as a mere property

93 *face* brazen

94 *Advise you* be careful

97 *bibble-babble*. There may be some echo here of a con-

troversy which raged round the preacher John Darrell, who claimed to have successfully cured several people possessed by devils. In 1600 Darrell published *A True Narration*, in which the victims are said on three occasions to have called the Scriptures 'bible-bable'. But the expression was quite a common one.

100 *God buy you* God be with you

102 *I will, sir, I will* (with a pun on 'marry' used as a mild oath and as meaning 'wed')

104 *shent* scolded

109 *Well-a-day!* alas!

121–8 *I am gone, sir, and anon, sir . . . goodman devil.* This may have been recited and not sung.

123 *old Vice* (a character who defied the devil in the early Tudor interludes which developed from the Morality plays. He was one ancestor of the Elizabethan stage fool.)

127 *Pare thy nails.* A passage in *Henry V* – 'this roaring devil i'th'old play, that everyone may pare his nails with a wooden dagger' (IV.4.69–70) – suggests that this was a familiar piece of stage business.

IV.3.6 *there he was* he had been there

credit report

11 *accident* unexpected happening

12 *instance* example

discourse reasoning

17 *sway* rule

18 *Take and give back affairs and their dispatch.* Olivia receives reports from her household and gives them orders in return.

21 *deceivable* deceptive

24 *chantry by* nearby chapel (a chantry being an endowed chapel where masses were said for the soul of the founder)

26 *Plight me the full assurance.* A ceremony of betrothal, in

the presence of a priest, was as binding a contract as the actual marriage service.

29 *Whiles* until

31 *birth* nobility

V.1.5–6 *This is to give a dog ... dog again.* Manningham's diary, which records the first known performance of *Twelfth Night*, also gives us the source of this saying: 'Mr Francis Curle told me how one Doctor Bulleyn, the Queen's kinsman, had a dog which he doted on, so much that the Queen, understanding of it, requested he would grant her one desire, and he should have whatsoever he would ask. She demanded his dog. He gave it, and – "Now, Madam," quoth he, "you promised to give me my desire." "I will," quoth she. "Then I pray you, give me my dog again."'

8 *trappings* bits and pieces. Feste, who belongs to no one, is irritated by Orsino's tone.

19–21 *conclusions to be as kisses, if your four negatives make your two affirmatives.* Similar jests of the period are based on the assumption that a girl's 'No, no, no, no!' could be interpreted as 'Yes, yes!'

27 *double-dealing* (punning on the meanings 'a double donation' and 'duplicity')

30 *your grace.* There is a pun here on (1) the form of address to a duke, and (2) Orsino's share of divine grace which should prevent his listening to 'ill counsel'.

34 *Primo, secundo, tertio* one, two, three (Latin for first, second, third – probably the beginning of a children's counting game)

35 *the third pays for all.* The words 'at this throw' in Orsino's next speech, meaning 'this throw of the dice', suggest that Feste is here quoting the gambler's proverb which is best known in the form 'third time lucky'.

36 *Saint Bennet* Saint Benedict. Shakespeare may have

been thinking of the London church just across the river from the Globe.

lullaby to your bounty may your generosity sleep well (continuing the metaphor used by Orsino)

46 *anon* soon

50 *Vulcan* (the smith of the gods in Roman mythology)

51 *baubling* paltry

52 *unprizable* worthless

53 *scatheful* destructive

54 *bottom* ship

55 *loss* the losers

58 *fraught* cargo

Candy Candia (now Crete)

61 *desperate of shame and state* recklessly disregarding both the harm a quarrel would do to his character and the danger in which it would place him

62 *brabble* brawl

64 *put strange speech upon me* spoke to me in a strange manner

65 *distraction* madness

68 *dear* dire

77 *wrack* shipwrecked person

79 *retention* power of holding back

81 *pure* purely, only

86 *face me out of* deny to my face

87 *removèd thing* estranged being

97 *Three months.* Actually Viola has been only three days in Orsino's service when she is sent to Olivia, and after that the action is very rapid. But the inconsistency passes unnoticed in the theatre.

104 *Good, my lord* (a polite request to Orsino to let Viola speak first)

107 *fat and fulsome* nauseating

111 *ingrate* ungrateful

114 *become him* be fitting for him

116 *th'Egyptian thief.* This alludes to a story told by Heliodorus in his *Ethiopica*, which was popular in a translation

in Shakespeare's day. The thief was Thyamis, a brigand who attempted to kill his captive Chariclea to prevent her falling into the hands of his own captors.

119 *non-regardance* contempt

121 *screws* wrenches

124 *tender* hold, esteem

126 *in his master's spite* to the mortification of his master

134 *More by all mores* more beyond all comparisons

137 *detested* denounced with an oath, execrated

143 *sirrah* (a contemptuous mode of address)

145 *strangle thy propriety* suppress your identity as my husband (perhaps with a play on a further meaning of *propriety*, 'ownership' – 'the fact that I am yours')

163 *a grizzle* grey hairs

case skin

165 *trip*. This can mean 'headlong speed' or 'trap', and probably means both here; Orsino calls Cesario both a deceiver and a fast worker.

169 *little* a little

171 *presently* at once

174 *coxcomb* pate

178–9 *incardinate* (Sir Andrew's error for 'incarnate')

181 *'Od's lifelings . . . !* God's life!

188 *set nothing by* think nothing of

189 *halting* limping

191 *othergates* otherwise

196 *set* closed

197 *passy-measures pavin*. This was a stately dance to a strain consisting of at least eight semibreves, and Sir Toby, an expert on the dance, is perhaps reminded of it by mention of 'eight i' the morning'. He means that Dick Surgeon's slowness in answering his call passes all measure. The phrase must have been a little puzzling to the copyist or compositor, because *pavin* appears as 'panyn' in the Folio. A more common form of the word is 'pavane'.

201–2 *be dressed* have our wounds dressed

203 *coxcomb* blockhead

204 *gull* fool

207 *the brother of my blood* my own brother

208 *with wit and safety* having any sense at all of my own safety

213 *habit* garb

214 *perspective* optical device. This could not have been a stereoscopic device, as these were not invented until the early eighteenth century. Besides, a stereoscopic device makes two images into one, and what Shakespeare has in mind here is something that makes one image into two. It could be a trick painting on a surface folded concertina-wise, so that it appeared to be two different paintings when viewed from two different angles. Or it could be a theatrical illusion of the Pepper's Ghost type in which, by the use of mirrors, one figure was turned into two. Such illusions were known and practised on the Continent early in the seventeenth century.

218 *Fear'st* do you doubt

224 *that deity in my nature* (ubiquity; only God can be in two places at once)

231 *suited* dressed

232–3 *If spirits can assume both form and suit | You come to fright us.* One Elizabethan theory about ghosts was that they were evil spirits assuming the appearance of dead people.

234 *dimension* bodily form

grossly substantially

235 *participate* have in common with others

236 *as the rest goes even* as everything fits in with your being my sister

243 *record* recollection

246 *lets* hinders

249 *cohere* accord together

jump agree

252 *weeds* clothes

257 *to her bias drew* obeyed her inclination (a metaphor from the game of bowls)

260 *maid and man* virgin youth

262 *as yet the glass seems true* as in fact the 'perspective' turns out not to be an illusion after all

263 *wrack* shipwreck

268 *that orbèd continent* (the sphere of the sun)

272 *action* legal charge

273 *durance* imprisonment

275 *enlarge* free

277 *distract* disturbed in his mind

278 *extracting* that drew everything else out of my thoughts. Olivia is playing a variation upon 'distract' in the previous line.

281–2 *Beelzebub at the stave's end* the devil at bay

284 *epistles.* Feste puns on the general sense 'letters' and the special sense 'New Testament letters'. There is a reference to the sixteenth-century liturgical controversies about when the gospel for the day should be read, or 'delivered'.

skills not doesn't matter

287–8 *delivers* speaks the words of

293 *vox* the right voice. This was a technical term of Elizabethan public speaking.

294 *Prithee* I pray thee (equivalent to 'please')

296 *perpend* be attentive

316 *proper* own

317 *apt* ready

318 *quits you* releases you from service

330 *from it* differently

331 *invention* composition

333 *in the modesty of honour* with a modest regard for your reputation

334 *lights* signals, indications

337 *lighter* lesser

341 *geck and gull* butt and dupe

344 *character* hand

348 *presupposed* previously enjoined

350 *This practice hath most shrewdly passed upon thee* this trick has been very cunningly played on you

359–60 *Upon some stubborn and uncourteous parts | We had conceived against him* in consequence of his stiff-necked and unfriendly behaviour to which we took exception

361 *importance* importunity

367 *poor fool!* (said affectionately)

baffled treated shamefully

374 *whirligig* spinning top

375 *pack* (a word used of a group of plotters)

379 *convents* calls us together

386 *When that I was and a little tiny boy.* The confusion of the fourth stanza suggests that this was a folk-song. Another stanza of it is said or sung by the Fool in *King Lear*. Modern actors of Feste like to sing it with pathos, but probably it was intended as a 'jig' or cheerful conclusion to a comedy. See page 205 for the tune to which it is traditionally sung in the theatre.

388 *toy* trifle

400 *tosspots* sots

AN ACCOUNT OF THE TEXT

Twelfth Night was first published in the posthumous collection of Shakespeare's plays known as the Folio (1623). It appears there in a very accurate and carefully-punctuated text in which misreadings such as 'coole my nature' (for 'curl by nature', I.3.94–5) are rare. The play's real puzzles, Mistress Mall's picture and the Lady of the Strachy, are not due to textual corruption but to our ignorance of Elizabethan gossip.

The manuscript of *Twelfth Night* which was sent to the printer in 1623 was either the copy of the play actually used for productions, known as the promptbook, or a copy of this specially made for the printer. This is evident from the theatrical practicality of the text as it stands. Actors' entrances are given at the point where they must begin to move on to the stage. For example, at V.1.186 Sir Toby starts to struggle in, supported by Feste. Sir Andrew speaks a sentence before he becomes aware of Sir Toby's arrival, and it takes another two lines spoken by Sir Andrew for Sir Toby to get well down-stage where Orsino can address him. So, too, the actor playing Malvolio is warned to get ready for the 'dark house' dialogue by the stage direction *Maluolio within*. Exits are not given when it is perfectly plain to the actor that he has to get off the stage. Thus Maria is kept flitting to and fro on errands, but the list of variant stage directions given below shows that most of her exits go unnoted. Nor does Malvolio need any direction to stalk out at 'I'll be revenged on the whole pack of you' (V.1.375), for it is evident from Orsino's next speech that he has done so.

An author's own 'fair copy' could be used as the promptbook in an Elizabethan theatre. Unfortunately there appears to be no evidence that this was the case with *Twelfth Night*. A small piece of evidence that the promptbook was not Shakespeare's fair copy is afforded by the occurrence of *Uiolenta* for *Viola* at I.5.160, *Marian* for *Maria* at II.3.13, and (unless a joke is intended) *Agueface* for *Aguecheek* at I.3.40. Such uncertainty about names is natural in the first Act or so of an autograph play, especially one that has been written in haste, but it is likely to be eliminated when the author copies out his work for himself. It is reasonably safe to assume that the manuscript of *Twelfth Night* which reached the playhouse presented the play in a finished form but was not tidy enough to be used as the promptbook, so that a copy had to be made. The possibility that Maria's letter is a stage closer to Shakespeare's autograph manuscript than is the rest of the play is briefly discussed in the Commentary, in notes on II.5.140 and on III.4.71.

The Act and scene divisions of the Folio are unlikely to be Shakespeare's own. They are quite arbitrary, and the action of the play is in fact continuous between Acts I and II, and between Acts III and IV. Possibly the Act divisions were introduced to give an opportunity for intermission music at Court performances, such as those in 1618 and 1623. In addition to these Act and scene divisions, which are in Latin, the Folio has *Finis Actus primus* (*secundus, Quartus*) at the end of Acts I, II, and IV. Other changes which may have been made in the play while it was in the King's Men's repertory are discussed in the Introduction.

The variants listed below do not include the few lines printed as prose in the Folio and as verse in this edition (for example, the 'Jolly Robin' song in IV.2) or the few others, such as III.4.19–22, which were erroneously printed in the Folio as verse but are here restored to prose. Following the practice of the Folio, a number of short verse-lines have been printed on their own, instead of being shown as halves of lines divided between two speakers, the normal practice of eighteenth- and nineteenth-century editions. Metrical continuity is natural only when one character is responding fully to another, either in affection or anger. When a character follows his or her own thoughts independently of the other speaker (as Viola does in I.2), or when a marked pause or sudden change of mood occurs, Shakespeare does not hesitate to use half-lines, and this edition has tried to preserve his free handling of his poetic medium. On the same principle, no attempt has been made to regularize lines such as 'That – methought – her eyes had lost her tongue' (II.2.20). The slight pause before and after the parenthesis lengthens out the line to a normal blank verse, and similar irregularities in other lines can usually be justified in the same way.

It will be seen from the short list of variants below that this is a very conservative text, preserving the Folio readings wherever they make sense. But what is sense in the study is not always sense on the modern stage. The second list is therefore of emendations which producers may wish to adopt in the theatre for the sake of lucidity.

I

The following is a list of readings in the present text which are departures from the Folio text of 1623. The reading on the right of the square bracket is that of the Folio.

Title. TWELFTH] Twelfe

I.1. 11 sea, naught] Sea. Nought
I.2. 15 Arion] *Orion*
I.3. 26 all, most] almost
49 SIR ANDREW] *Ma.*
94–5 curl by nature] coole my nature
128 dun-coloured] dam'd colour'd
set] sit
131 That's] That
I.5. 86 guiltless] guitlesse
142 He's] Ha's
160 (stage direction) *Viola*] *Uiolenta*
II.2. 31 our frailty] O frailtie
II.3. 2 *diluculo*] *Deliculo*
24 leman] Lemon
25 impetticoat] impeticos

II.3	83	O' the twelfth] O the twelfe
	130	a nayword] an ayword
	142	swathes] swarths
II.5.	112	staniel] stallion
	140	born] become
	141	achieve] atcheeues
	154	champain] champian
	169	dear] deero
III.1.	8	king] Kings
	66	wise men, folly-fallen] wisemens folly falne
	88	all ready] already
III.2.	7	see thee the] see the
	50	thy] the
	63	nine] mine
	66	renegado] Renegatho
III.4.	23	OLIVIA] *Mal.*
	71	tang] langer
	289	oath's sake] oath sake
IV.2.	7	student] Studient
	14	Gorboduc] Gorbodacke
	37	clerestories] cleere stores
	51	haply] happily
IV.3.	27	jealous] jealious
V.1.	173	He's] H'as
		he's] has
	193	he's] has
	197	pavin] panyn

2

The following is a list of well-founded emendations which have not been adopted in this edition. The emendation is in each case to the right of the square bracket.

I.1.	5	sound] south
	27	heat] hence
I.2.	40–41	sight | And company] company | And sight

I.3. 39 *vulgo*] *volto*
128 dun-coloured] flame-coloured
I.4. 33 shrill and sound] shrill of sound
I.5. 191 not mad] but mad
197–8 Tell me your mind; I am a messenger] OLIVIA Tell me your mind. VIOLA I am a messenger
II.2. 12 of me, I'll none] of me! I'll none
20 That – methought –] That sure methought
32 made, if such] made of, such
II.3. 9 lives] life
144 grounds] ground
II.4. 52 Fie away, fie away] Fly away, fly away
87 It] I
II.5. 33 SIR TOBY] FABIAN
37 SIR TOBY] FABIAN
169–70 dear my sweet] dear, O my sweet
III.2. 50 cubiculo] cubicle
III.3. 15 And thanks. And ever oft] And thanks and ever thanks. And oft
III.4. 88 How is't with you, man?] SIR TOBY How is't with you, man?
198 unchary on't] unchary out
203 griefs] grief
241 computent] competent
346 lying, vainness] lying vainness
IV.2. 69–70 the upshot] to the upshot
V.1. 112 have] hath
369 thrown] thrust

3

There follow the chief departures of this edition from the Folio stage directions. Minor additions such as *aside*, *reads*, *sings*, *to Feste*, are not noted here.

I.1. 1 *Music*] not in F
I.5. 1 *Feste the Clown*] *Clowne* here and elsewhere throughout the Folio

I.5. 28 *and attendants*] not in F
124 *followed by Maria*] not in F
133 *Exit*] not in F
194 (*showing Viola the way out*)] not in F
210 *Maria and attendants withdraw*] not in F
301 *Exit*] *Finis, Actus primus.* F

II.2. 41 *Exit*] not in F

II.4. 14 *Exit Curio*] not in F
78 *Curio and attendants withdraw*] not in F

II.5. 20 *The men hide. Maria throws down a letter*] not in F
200 *Exeunt*] *Exeunt. Finis Actus secundus* F

III.1. 1 *at different entrances ... playing his pipe and tabor*] not in F
42 *She gives him a coin*] not in F
52 *She gives another coin*] not in F
80 *Maria*] *Gentlewoman* F
90 *Exeunt Sir Toby ... he, too, leaves*] not in F

III.2. 80 *Exeunt*] *Exeunt Omnes.* F

III.3. 49 *separately*] not in F

III.4. 14 *Exit Maria*] not in F
15 *and Maria*] not in F
64 *and Maria different ways*] not in F
196 *Exit Maria. Sir Toby and Fabian stand aside*] not in F
213 *Sir Toby and Fabian come forward*] *Enter Toby and Fabian.* F
266 F gives direction *Exeunt* for Viola and Fabian
282 (*Aside, as he crosses to Fabian*)] not in F
283 (*To Fabian*)] *Enter Fabian and Viola.*
296 (*crossing to Sir Andrew*)] not in F
301 *He draws*] not in F. So too *She draws* at line 302.
363 *Exeunt Antonio and Officers*] *Exit* F
375 *Exit*] not in F
384 *Exit*] not in F
386 *Exeunt*] *Exit* F

IV.1. 24 *He strikes Sebastian*] not in F

IV.1. 25 *He beats Sir Andrew with the handle of his dagger*] not in F
31 *He grips Sebastian*] not in F
40 *He breaks free and draws his sword*] not in F
43 *He draws*] not in F
50 *Exeunt Sir Toby, Sir Andrew, and Fabian*] not in F

IV.2. 3 *Exit*] not in F
10 *and Maria*] not in F
70 *and Maria*] not in F
95 (*In priest's voice*)] not in F. So in line 101.
99–100 (*In own voice*)] not in F. So in line 101.

IV.3. 35 *Exeunt*] *Exeunt. Finis Actus Quartus.* F

V.1. 140 *Exit an attendant*] not in F
205 *Exeunt Sir Toby and Sir Andrew, helped by Feste and Fabian*] not in F
288 *He reads frantically*] not in F
298 (*snatching the letter and giving it to Fabian*)] not in F
312 *Exit Fabian*] not in F
323 *and Fabian*] not in F
375 *Exit*] not in F
385 *all but Feste*] not in F
405 *Exit*] FINIS F

THE SONGS

The editor gratefully acknowledges the assistance of F. W. Sternfeld in the transcribing and editing of the songs.

1. 'O mistress mine' (II.3.37)

No contemporary setting has survived, but there exist two instrumental pieces with this title, both based on the same tune. Their exact relationship to the song in the play is not known, but the tune can be fitted to Shakespeare's words. The words, the tune, or both, may be traditional. The song printed below has been transcribed and edited by Sidney Beck from Thomas Morley's *First Book of Consort Lessons*, published in 1599.

2. 'Hold thy peace' (II.3.63)

This round was published in Thomas Ravenscroft's *Deuteromelia*, 1609.

3. 'Three merry men' (II.3.75)

The following version of this catch has been transcribed and edited from William Lawes's *Catch that Catch Can*, 1652. The tune may go back to Shakespeare's time.

4. 'There dwelt a man in Babylon' (II.3.78)

This is the first line of 'The Ballad of Constant Susanna', which was sung to a corrupt version of 'Greensleeves'.

5. 'O' the twelfth day of December' (II.3.83)

No early music is known.

6. 'Farewell, dear heart' (II.3.99)

This song by Robert Jones was printed in his *First Book of Airs*, 1600. It has been transcribed and adapted to the words of the play.

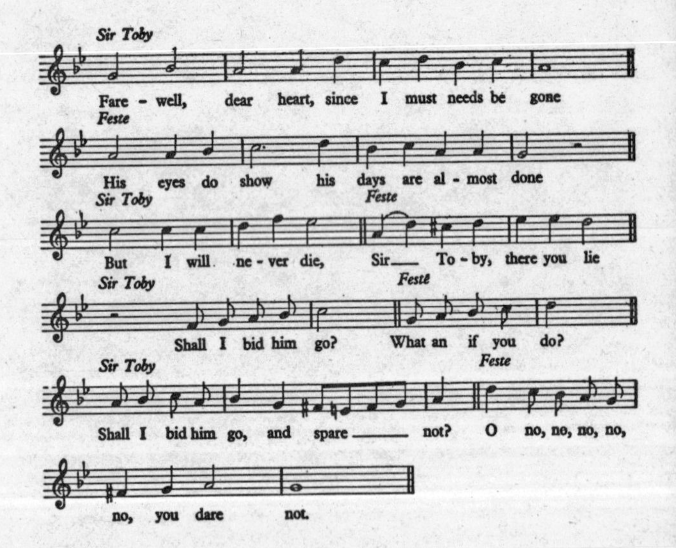

7. 'Come away, come away death' (II.4.50)
No early music is known.

8. 'Hey Robin' (IV.2.71)

This is part of a round for three or four voices, probably by William Corneyshe (*c.* 1465–*c.* 1523), preserved in the British Museum, Additional MSS. 31922 (sixteenth century; folios 53–4). The full round, transcribed and edited, is given below. It is followed by an arrangement suitable for stage performance.

15
thou shalt know of
mine.
Hey Ro - bin,
Jol - ly Ro -
thou shalt know of
mine.
Hey Ro - bin,
Jol - ly Ro -
thou shalt know of
mine.
Hey Ro - bin,
Jol - ly Ro -
20
- bin!
Tell me how thy
le - man doth and
thou shalt know of
- bin!
Tell me how thy
le - man doth and
thou shalt know of
- bin!
Tell me how thy
le - man doth and
thou shalt know of
24
mine.
1. My
2. I
la - dy is un -
can - not think such
kind per-dy, A -
doub - le - ness For
lack why is she
I find wo - man
mine.
Hey Ro - bin,
Jol - ly Ro -
mine.
Hey Ro - bin,
Jol - ly Ro -

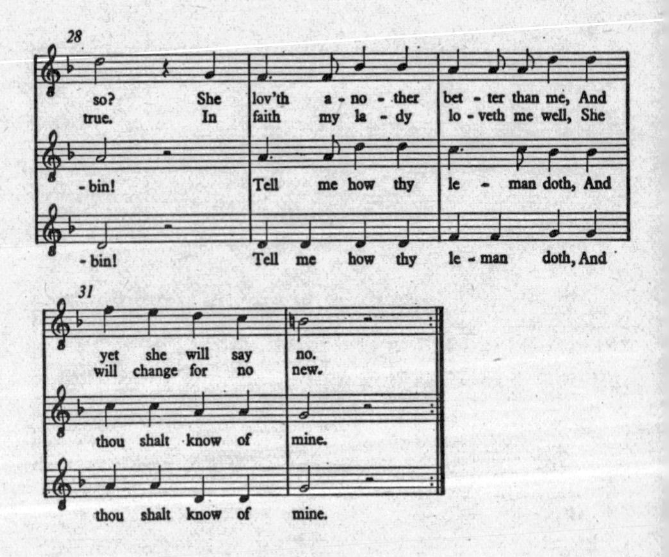
28
so? She lov'th a - no - ther bet - ter than me, And
true. In faith my la - dy lo - veth me well, She
- bin! Tell me how thy le - man doth, And
- bin! Tell me how thy le - man doth, And
31
yet she will say no.
will change for no new.
thou shalt know of mine.
thou shalt know of mine.

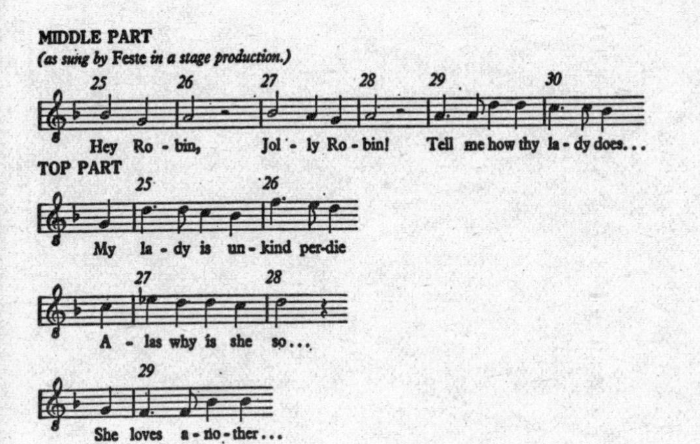
MIDDLE PART
(as sung by Feste in a stage production.)
25 26 27 28 29 30
Hey Ro - bin, Jol - ly Ro - bin! Tell me how thy la - dy does...
TOP PART
25 26
My la - dy is un - kind per-die
27 28
A - las why is she so...
29
She loves a - no - ther...

9. 'I am gone, sir' (IV.2.121)

No early music has survived.

10. 'When that I was and a little tiny boy' (V.1.386)

The tune to which these lines are traditionally sung first appears in a volume called *The New Songs in the Pantomime of the Witches; the Celebrated Epilogue in the Comedy of Twelfth Night . . . sung by Mr Vernon at Vauxhall; composed by J. Vernon*, and printed in 1772. It may be an arrangement of a traditional melody. The version printed below is based on William Chappell's *Popular Music of the Olden Time* (1859), where the source is not identified.

An accompaniment by F. W. Sternfeld is printed in his *Songs from Shakespeare's Tragedies* (Oxford University Press, 1964).

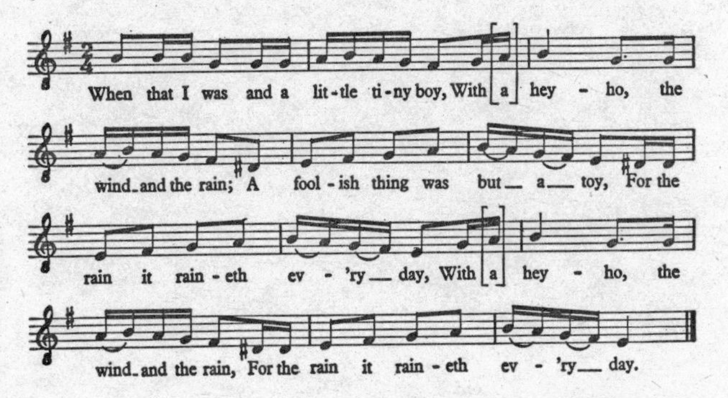

MORE ABOUT PENGUINS AND PELICANS

For further information about books available from Penguins please write to Dept EP, Penguin Books Ltd, Harmondsworth, Middlesex UB7 ODA.

In the U.S.A.: For a complete list of books available from Penguins in the United States write to Dept CS, Penguin Books, 625 Madison Avenue, New York, New York 10022.

In Canada: For a complete list of books available from Penguins in Canada write to Penguin Books Canada Ltd, 2801 John Street, Markham, Ontario L3R 1B4.

In Australia: For a complete list of books available from Penguins in Australia write to the Marketing Department, Penguin Books Australia Ltd, P.O. Box 257, Ringwood, Victoria 3134.

NEW PENGUIN SHAKESPEARE

General Editor: T. J. B. Spencer

All's Well That Ends Well Barbara Everett
Antony and Cleopatra Emrys Jones
As You Like It H. J. Oliver
The Comedy of Errors Stanley Wells
Coriolanus G. R. Hibbard
Hamlet T. J. B. Spencer
Henry IV, Part 1 P. H. Davison
Henry IV, Part 2 P. H. Davison
Henry V A. R. Humphreys
Henry VI, Part 1 Norman Sanders
Henry VI, Part 2 Norman Sanders
Henry VI, Part 3 Norman Sanders
Henry VIII A. R. Humphreys
Julius Caesar Norman Sanders
King John R. L. Smallwood
King Lear G. K. Hunter
Macbeth G. K. Hunter
Measure for Measure J. M. Nosworthy
The Merchant of Venice W. Moelwyn Merchant
The Merry Wives of Windsor G. R. Hibbard
A Midsummer Night's Dream Stanley Wells
Much Ado About Nothing R. A. Foakes
Othello Kenneth Muir
Pericles Philip Edwards
The Rape of Lucrece J. W. Lever
Richard II Stanley Wells
Richard III E. A. J. Honigmann
Romeo and Juliet T. J. B. Spencer
The Taming of the Shrew G. R. Hibbard
The Tempest Anne Righter (Anne Barton)
Timon of Athens G. R. Hibbard
The Two Gentlemen of Verona Norman Sanders
The Two Noble Kinsmen N. W. Bawcutt
The Winter's Tale Ernest Schanzer